I0623651

The Longest Day II

The Eden Stories

TERRY TOLER

The Longest Day II
Published by: BeHoldings, LLC

Copyright © 2023, **BeHoldings, LLC**
Terry Toler
All rights reserved.

All rights reserved. No part of this publication may be reproduced, stored in a retrieval system, or transmitted in any form, or by any means—electronic, mechanical, photocopying, recording or otherwise—without prior written permission.

Book Cover: BeHoldings Publishing
Contributing Editor: Donna Toler

For information email: terry@terrytoler.com.

Our books can be purchased in bulk for promotional, educational, and business use. Please contact your bookseller or the BeHoldings Publishing Sales department at:sales@terrytoler.com

For booking information email: booking@terrytoler.com.
First U.S. Edition: February, 2023

Printed in the United States of America
ISBN 978-1-954710-19-1

This is a work of fiction. All of the characters, organizations, and events portrayed in this novel are either products of the author's imagination or are used fictitiously. Any resemblance to actual persons, living or dead is entirely coincidental.

OTHER BOOKS BY TERRY TOLER

Fiction

The Longest Day

The Reformation of Mars

The Late, Great Planet Jupiter

The Great Wall of Ven-Us

Saturn: The Eden Experiment

The Mercury Protocols

Save The Girls

The Ingenue

Saving Sara

Save The Queen

No Girl Left Behind

The Launch

Body Count

Save Me Twice

Powerful Enemies

Deadly Games

Don't Be Careful

Wintervention

Cliff Hangers: Anna

Cliff Hangers: Mr. & Mrs. Platt

Cliff Hangers: The Quarterback

Cliff Hangers: Macy

Cliff Hangers: Not, Not Guilty

Cliff Hangers: The Book Club

Cliff Hangers: The Book Club Murder

The Blue Rose

Triggers

Non-Fiction

How to Make More Than a Million Dollars
The Heart Attacked
Seven Years of Promise
Mission Possible
Marriage Made in Heaven
21 Days to Physical Healing
21 Days to Spiritual Fitness
21 Days to Divine Health
21 Days to a Great Marriage
21 Days to Financial Freedom
21 Days to Sharing Your Faith
21 Days to Mission Possible
7 Days to Emotional Freedom
Uncommon Finances
Uncommon Health
Uncommon Marriage
The Jesus Diet
Suddenly Free
Feeling Free

For more information on these books and other resources visit
terrytoler.com.

Thank you for purchasing this novel from best-selling author Terry Toler. As an additional thank you, Terry wants to give you a free gift.

Sign up for:

Updates
New Releases
Announcements

At terrytoler.com

We'll send you an eBook, *The Book Club*, a Cliff Hangers novella, free of charge. The one that started the Cliff Ford mysteries.

Inspired by True Events

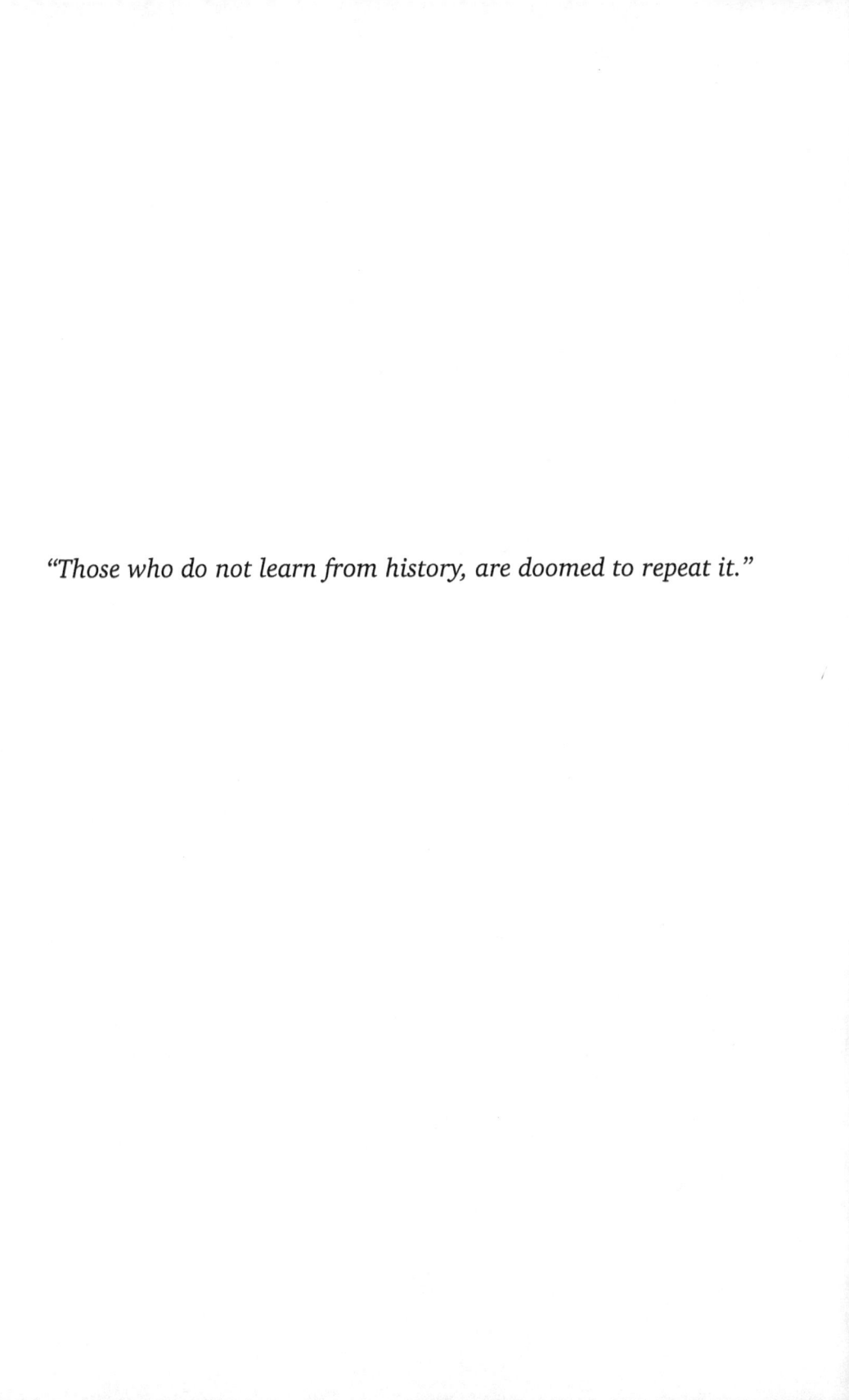

"Those who do not learn from history, are doomed to repeat it."

1

Thirty years later

The whole thing had been a dream. A nightmare actually.

Adam Lange felt relief. He thought he had traveled to the ends of the universe and discovered a perfect planet named Adon. One in which Adam and Eve hadn't eaten from the tree of the knowledge of good and evil.

It all seemed so real. The hundreds of years in space. The fire that severely burned his body. Almost killed him.

Landing on the planet. Discovering life. Meeting the prophet Elias who healed him.

Meeting Adam and Eve.

Meeting God.

God seemed so real. Of course, Adam was an atheist. He didn't believe in God.

Adam was surprised Courtney was willing to marry him. She was such a devout Christian.

The wedding chapel was packed. He stood at the front looking deeply into Courtney's eyes as the minister spoke.

The words were a blur.

He'd never been more in love than at that moment.

In his dream he'd been in love with Lucy. Another astronaut who was in training to follow Adam into space, a few years after he left on his one-way journey. Adam saw her yesterday at training. That must've been why she was in his dream.

Am I still going?

Of course not. That trip wasn't going to happen now. Astronauts couldn't be a part of the program if married or had kids. He chose Courtney over his career. Gave up everything he worked so hard for.

Why would he do that? He always thought of himself as a career bachelor.

Why was he thinking about Lucy at that moment? Did he have feelings for her? Should he be getting married if he did.

Panic flowed through his body like jet fuel through a spacecraft. Adam fought to get the images of Lucy out of his head.

He had kissed her. Several times. *Was that cheating?*

Courtney frowned. Like she knew what he was thinking.

The last kiss with Lucy was in the Garden of Eden. On Adon.

Something went wrong. Something horrible.

Lucy enticed him to eat from the tree of the knowledge of good and evil.

He did it.

God was angry. Adam remembered it. It caused him to shudder.

The people of Adon were kicked out of the garden. Then it disappeared altogether. Adam and Eve were murdered.

Adam felt so ashamed. It was all his fault.

Thank God it was only a dream.

Why was he thanking God? He didn't believe in God.

The minister interrupted his thoughts.

"Do you Adam, take Courtney to be your lawfully wedded wife, to have and to hold from this day forward, for better or for worse, in sickness and in health, for as long as you both shall live? So help you God?"

"Can you rephrase the question?" Adam asked. "I don't believe in God."

Courtney grimaced. Adam recomposed himself.

He looked directly in Courtney's eyes and said emphatically, "I do."

"You may now kiss your bride."

Did she already do her vows? The whole thing was happening so fast. He didn't remember.

Didn't matter.

Adam took Courtney in his arms, and they began to kiss. Slowly at first, and then passionately as the friends and family in the audience applauded and cheered loudly.

Adam felt something on his face. He pulled back from Courtney and reached to wipe it off.

Blood . . . coming from Courtney's mouth. *What?*

Jamie was the maid of honor. His daughter Jamie Austen. Adam could see her out of the corner of his eye. She let out a blood curdling scream as Courtney's face began to contort. Fangs began protruding out of her elongated mouth. Courtney's body grew to twenty plus feet as her arms morphed into wings and began flailing around.

Sarge ran toward Courtney and tried to grab her, but she swatted him away, throwing him across the room and into the wall. He crumbled into a heap.

A diabolical laugh echoed through the church and rang through Adam's head as people started running, trampling each other, turning over chairs, desperately trying to get away. Adam tried to run but his legs wouldn't move.

The same thing had happened to Lucy in his dream. She had turned into a monster. The evil one. He'd been tricked.

Courtney is the serpent too . . .

Adam shot straight up in his bed, shaking, and covered in sweat even though it was cool in the spacecraft. For the third time that week, he'd had the same dream. A nightmare he'd been living for thirty years.

2

Elias' son, Benjamin, was getting married and Adam promised he would be there. That's probably why he kept dreaming about a wedding. Funny he dreamed about Courtney. It'd been hundreds of years since he'd seen her.

Courtney was a psychologist with NASA back on earth. They'd never really dated. Only kissed once. The day before he left on that fateful journey.

If only he could go back in time. He would've never gotten on that spacecraft. Maybe he could've had a life with Courtney.

He had many regrets. Being an atheist at the top of the list. Considering he'd actually met God in the Garden of Eden.

How arrogant does one have to be to deny the existence of God?

He'd been so stupid. Eating from the tree of the knowledge of good and evil. The people of Adon would still be living their perfect existence. With the garden and with God.

Elias said God would work it all for good. Adam didn't see how that was possible. Elias was the prophet of God who laid hands on Adam and healed him. Right after he landed on Adon.

Adam had been badly burned in a fire on his spacecraft. That's the main reason he even landed on Adon. The fire destroyed his oxygen supply. He would've died within a few days, had he not somehow found that planet.

Everyone would've been better off if he had perished.

God had been so good to Adam.

Would he ever forgive me for what I did?

He didn't know. God was no longer on Adon. At least not visibly. They only heard his voice occasionally. He never talked to Adam. Adam would give anything to talk to God again. Explain what had happened.

He couldn't let himself think about it. He had to keep himself busy. Hard to do with his isolated existence. Living out of his spacecraft, Chronos. Alone. It'd been weeks since he'd been back to the Central City.

Going to the wedding would be a welcomed reprieve from the loneliness.

Elias was one of the only friends he had left.

The spacecraft was readied. Adam was meticulous in his routine. The ship had to be locked down securely, protected from looters ... and from Aza and his men who might try to break in as they had tried to do several times already.

Aza and one of his men were the ones who killed Adam and Eve. Thrust a knife and spear into them. Adam would've killed him by now, but God said he wasn't supposed to be touched. That anyone who killed Aza would receive vengeance seven times over.

What did it matter? Adam deserved punishment. Seven times over wouldn't be enough.

Adam had a different plan. What if he killed Aza in self-defense? Aza was actively trying to kill Adam. Surely God wouldn't care if Adam was only protecting himself.

Chronos had served as an impenetrable fortress. Adam rarely ventured out and only when necessary. He felt safe there. Nowhere in Adon was safe anymore, even in the daylight.

He rarely went to Adon. It only reminded him all of this was his fault. He had eaten the apple. Brought sin and death to Adon.

Unimaginable suffering. He'd wanted to end his life more times than he could count. Elias said God had a purpose for his life. That the people of Adon needed him.

Would Elias think that if he knew the truth?

Knew that Adam was the one who had eaten the apple and brought destruction upon the people?

Adam felt power and dread as he wrapped his hand around the handgun he carried with him everywhere he went. A stainless-steel slide and a body of only six inches in length made it easy to conceal. The weapon of choice because of the small size but also for the high capacity to shoot off multiple rounds in quick succession in case follow up shots were needed.

Adam made sure it was fully loaded and a round chambered. The safety was turned off, the gun then placed in a holster attached to his belt under his shirt.

Hopefully, it wouldn't be needed, but Adam wasn't taking any chances.

He closed the hatch of the spacecraft and started up the hill to the entrance of Adon.

He went through the gate that hadn't been tended to in years, overgrown with weeds and thatches almost blocking the path. Adam paused at the overlook, staring remorsefully at the once majestic and perfect city now a desolate wasteland of destruction.

Adon was unrecognizable.

The lake that once bustled with children playing and animals frolicking in the water had completely dried up with only a small puddle in the middle. Adam longed to be able to sit on the edge of the lake and have children knock over his drink.

So many regrets.

No tiger was around to play fetch anymore. The animals had been driven out into the wilderness toward the eastern district as people began to hunt them for food and took their pelts for clothes. If anyone saw an animal in Adon, they had to quickly flee from it.

Adam had a weapon for protection against the wild animals. Most people didn't. The animals were starving as was most of the population. The bigger predators would sometimes snatch women and children and consume them for food.

Adam wandered through the destruction that was once-thriving neighborhoods, restaurants, buildings, and parks. The pristine lawns were now overgrown with weeds, and most of the houses were in disrepair.

He avoided the neighborhood where Adam and Eve's house had stood for thousands of years. The memories were too painful. Their house had been looted and abandoned then set on fire. Most houses were still lived in but were only a shell of their former glory.

A young child tugged on the back of Adam's shirt. She held out her hand, begging for food. Her face had a layer of grime that had dried and was caked on her cheeks. Her hair was matted and had obviously not been washed in weeks. Her eyes were distant and sad. She had a look of acceptance of her plight, although she had no idea why she had to live her life hungry.

Born in the wrong place at the wrong time. Had she been born fifty years earlier, she would've had a perfect life, for a while at least. By fate, or just bad luck, she was bound to a horrible existence.

She asked him for a piece of bread. Adam didn't have any bread, but he had a pill in a packet he pulled out and gave to her. She wouldn't know that it was the best thing he could give her. It had many vitamins and minerals that would help her for the moment, even if it wouldn't satisfy the hunger she felt every day.

The girl washed it down with some water Adam had brought with him. It broke his heart.

She had no idea that the man who was being so kind to her was the one responsible for her suffering. The cause of all the destruction.

A heavy weight for Adam to carry.

The people of Adon didn't deserve their fate. He deserved to be punished, not them. Not that child. She was an innocent whose life was different because Adam had been stupid.

He still couldn't believe he was so easily fooled by the wiles of a woman.

Lucy.

Adam should have known better, even though the serpent disguised himself as a woman. The things Lucy had been telling him didn't make sense. Looking back, he could see them clearly. No accent, even though she was from Boston. Her spacecraft getting there faster. Avoiding talking about Earth. Not wanting to meet the people of Adon. Refusing to let him see her spacecraft.

The red flags were there; he simply ignored them for what he thought was love. It wasn't love; it was lust.

He was tricked. Still, he had no excuse. He knew better than to eat the fruit even if he did desire the woman. He read the Bible and knew the consequences better than anyone. He wished he could go back in time and do it again. It haunted him day and night for more than three decades now.

He saw some men carrying a dead body covered in a sheet.

Death was everywhere in Adon. Sickness and disease were epidemic. Famine, plagues, murders, accidents, and suicides were taking many of their numbers daily.

Adam was lucky. The famine hadn't hit him. He still had hundreds of years of food left, and he'd managed to fix the water-making machine from some parts he looted from a store in the city.

Water was in short supply. All of Adon and the surrounding territories had become like deserts.

It only made him feel more guilt. He didn't have the guts to tell anyone it was him. No one knew it was his fault.

Adam stopped and stared at what was once the entrance to the Garden of Eden. The townspeople had built a small garden in its place and named it the Garden of Sorrows. Barely a patch, compared to the garden that was there before.

Across the way was the square where Adam and Eve were murdered. Many had been killed and many martyred since. Once murder entered the world, it became more commonplace.

Things got worse in Adon by the day. It took more than six thousand years for earth to destroy itself after the fall; Adon might do it in less than a hundred.

Zelbe, Aza's mother, had formed a ruthless government in the central city which slowly destroyed those who still served God. She led what she called a "sexual revolution." Promiscuity, adultery, and fornication were rampant and encouraged. Prostitutes were present in the temples she had built for herself and her husband. They enticed men and young boys to indulge in all manner of debauchery. Even with each other. Zelbe encouraged what she called sexual freedom and enlightenment.

Rumor was she frequently had orgies and wild parties at her palace. God had raised up prophets who spoke out against her behavior. They said Zelbe had traded the truth for a lie. Zelbe put to death prophets who spoke against her. She had almost attacked Adam when he called her a Jezebel.

Adam knew that she was a false prophet and that she must be resisted. The Zelbe on Adon was acting the same way the Jezebel in the Bible operated. The Bible mentioned a Jezebel spirit. Could a spirit from earth make it all the way to Adon? Perhaps that was why she reacted so strongly when she heard the name spoken.

The people in the central district of Adon had asked God for a king. God said he should be enough for them, but they insisted. So,

God let them choose, and they chose Joab, Zelbe's husband. Promises were made and not kept. The people had believed Joab when he said he would end the famine and drought and restore Adon to its former glory.

At first Joab and Zelbe warred with each other even though they were husband and wife. They both wanted power. At some point, they came together in an unholy alliance of convenience. They merged the eastern district with the central district and formed their government. Not really a government. More of a dictatorship. They created a currency with Zelbe's image on the coins.

Joab and Zelbe had seventeen sons before the fall. Those sons organized an army to keep the people under control. Aza, the son who had murdered Adam at the town square, was the heir apparent and would eventually become king. Aza and his brothers carried out her decrees and were charged with stamping down the rebellion.

The people had grown to regret asking God for a king. They hated the queen even more. She was the driving force behind the depravity and violence.

Zelbe was determined to find out who ate the apple and punish him or her. Aza was put in charge of that task. He was ruthless. He went from house to house interrogating innocent men and women. Those who challenged Aza were put in jail—or worse, put to death.

Aza was particularly cruel in his methods. Most were beaten and released. Some were burned at the stake. Others were fed to lions. The methods were designed to invoke the maximum amount of fear in people.

Aza and Adam had a running feud. Adam refused to worship their false gods, and he refused to recognize Joab and Zelbe as the authorities.

Adam kept one eye out for Aza and his men as he weaved his way through the city to Elias' house.

He rounded a corner.

His heart skipped a beat.

Aza and his soldiers were up ahead. Adam normally tried to avoid them, but they were right on the road to Elias' house. He hoped they wouldn't see him, but they did.

They blocked his path.

"Where are you going?" Aza said, roughly.

"None of your business."

Adam wasn't afraid of Aza.

The same wasn't true for Aza, who was terrified of Adam. Even if he tried not to show it in front of his men.

Adam wanted a confrontation. He wanted to kill Aza. Then hoped someone would put him out of his misery. Adam had no concern about his life other than the extent to which he could protect those who were innocent. The only thing that kept him going was his desire to try and help as many people as possible with food, water, and protection.

Aza knew that Adam was friends with Elias and the other prophets, but he could do nothing about it. He was afraid of the people. The oppressed citizens of Adon were easily controlled. Aza didn't want to give them anything that might motivate them to overthrow his power.

Adam tried to provoke Aza. Maybe this was the time he could force a confrontation. Adam began to mock him.

"Why don't you run home to your momma, Aza you scum?" Adam said.

Aza drew his sword when Adam took a step towards him. One of Aza's soldiers held his arm and said, "His time is coming."

Aza said, "I'm watching you. I know you're the one who ate the apple. I can't prove it. But when I do, I'm going to revel in watching you die a slow death at my hand. Be careful walking out here at night. I want to be the one who kills you."

Aza was right. It had become very dangerous to walk at night. Adam was always on the lookout, especially if he was alone. He touched the weapon at his side, as if to make sure it was still there.

"You don't know anything," Adam said. "You're the one who'd better watch his back. You're forgetting I have weapons that can kill you in an instant."

Several years ago, Aza had brought a group of soldiers to search Adam's spacecraft. Adam fought them off with an automatic rifle, killing several of Aza's soldiers. The soldiers had been afraid of Adam ever since. Their knives and swords were no match for the semiautomatic gun Adam was carrying.

Adam knew he wouldn't need it. Aza was more talk than substance. He talked bravely when his soldiers were around and could do the fighting for him. If he and Adam were alone in a dark alley, Adam had no doubt he would whimper like a little baby and run away at the first chance.

"You've been warned," Aza said. "So has Elias. I'm watching him as well."

Adam drew his gun and said angrily, "You stay away from Elias. If you touch him, you will answer to me."

Aza and his soldiers quickly backed away. They left as fast as they could to get away from the gun.

Adam knew he would see them again.

3

Elias and his wife, Sophie, greeted Adam warmly. Their son Benjamin came running from another room to greet him. Adam gave him a hearty hug.

"Congratulations, Benjamin," Adam said. "On your nuptials."

"What are nuptials?" he asked.

Adam laughed. "It's a term on Earth. It simply means wedding. Congratulations on your wedding. You're a lucky man."

Adam had met Benjamin's bride-to-be many times and was impressed by her. Although he questioned the wisdom of getting married considering the state of the planet. Everyone needed to focus on surviving. He hoped they weren't considering bringing children into the world.

Adam hadn't expressed those feelings to Elias or to Benjamin and wasn't about to say anything to risk ruining the broad smile on Benjamin's face.

"I am a lucky man," Benjamin said. "I can't wait to be married."

"Here's the best advice I can give you," Adam said. "Admit when you're wrong, and don't say anything when you're right."

Not that he knew. Adam was never married. Except in his nightmares.

Somehow, he remembered that joke from when he was on earth. Hundreds of years ago. So much of his time on earth kept flooding his memories. Causing him to long for those simpler times.

Of course, he would've died centuries ago. Only lived another thirty or forty years longer on earth. If he had a choice, he'd choose that option compared to this.

Benjamin had a frown on his face. "I don't understand what you mean. Why shouldn't I say anything if I'm right?"

"You'll know soon enough, son," Elias said, with a sly grin on his face.

Sophie patted her husband on the chest. "I wish your father would take that advice."

Elias' grin got bigger. "If I'm ever wrong, I'll admit it," he said. "It just hasn't happened yet."

He let out a deep and boisterous laugh. Sophie rolled her eyes. Then slapped him on the chest. A little harder the second time.

"I'm going to check on the food," she said, as she disappeared from the room before anyone could respond.

"I have a feeling you'll be saying you're sorry for that remark later tonight," Adam quipped.

Elias furrowed his brow, and his tone turned more serious. "Funny you should say that. I find myself saying I'm sorry more often these days. Sophie and I have been married for thousands of years. Before the fall, we never spoke a single harsh word to each other. Ever since someone ate the fruit from the tree of the knowledge of good and evil in the Garden of Eden, we've had several serious disagreements. Sometimes I can't believe the words that come out of our mouths."

Adam grimaced on the inside. He held his face expressionless, trying desperately not to give anything away.

The whole conversation caused his insides to churn. Talking about the wedding reminded him of his nightmare. Elias bringing up the Garden of Eden caused his heart to sink to the bottom of his chest.

The guilt, shame, and condemnation overwhelmed him. So much so, he wanted to bolt out of the house and never come back.

He resisted the urge and pretended nothing was bothering him.

The fall.

Elias had used a new term. Adam had never heard it called that before. That only added to his pain. It felt more like a jump off a cliff than a fall.

"I'm so . . . rry," Adam said. His voice cracked.

Elias put his hand on Adam's shoulder.

"No. I'm sorry, my friend," Elias said. "It's not your fault."

Yes it is.

"I shouldn't have brought up the Garden of Eden. This is supposed to be a celebration. A wedding. I'm the one who should apologize."

Adam waved his hand dismissively. "Don't apologize. You didn't cause all this."

"All have sinned and come short of the glory of God. We are all to blame in some ways."

"I suppose. It's been thirty years, but I remember that day like it was a few hours ago. I can't believe things have gotten so bad so quickly."

"Things are sure different. There's not much to celebrate on Adon. Weddings and the birth of a child are about the only things that bring families together to forget their troubles, if only for a moment. That's what I want to do now. Let's not ruin it for Benjamin with talk about the fall, the garden, and all our troubles."

"I'd better go find my bride," Benjamin said. If they had ruined his mood, you couldn't tell it in his demeanor.

"On Earth, the groom isn't allowed to see the bride before the wedding," Adam said, after he was gone.

"How does a man know he even wants to get married?" Elias asked. "If he's never seen her before."

Adam forced out a chuckle. "They've met before. It's called dating. It's on their wedding day that the groom isn't allowed to see the bride. It's supposedly bad luck."

"We don't want any bad luck. Things are bad enough as it is."

A pain shot through Adam's heart like a dart. This was one reason he didn't go out much. Too many reminders.

"It's only a superstition," Adam said, wishing he could find something to talk about that didn't remind him of his foolishness.

Elias noticed. He motioned for Adam to join him out on the back porch. Once there, he said, "You don't seem like yourself. How was your journey over here? Did you have any trouble?"

Adam felt relief. He could use his confrontation with Aza as an excuse for his strange behavior.

"Aza stopped me. But he wasn't going to harm me. He did threaten you, though. You need to be careful."

"We're all under threat. Joab and Zelbe are having prophets killed daily. Zelbe calls herself a prophetess. Yet, she worships Bel and has the real prophets of God killed."

"The people never should've made Joab king."

Elias nodded. "It's an abomination. Zelbe has appointed hundreds of false prophets to run the Temple. They wrote a set of laws and decrees the people must follow or be punished. One of them is that we must all bow down and worship the king and queen."

"I'm never doing that. No one should," Adam said, although he understood why others would succumb to the pressure.

"Obah was killed when he wouldn't bow down to her. She tried to hunt down Eli, but he escaped. She's still looking for him. She's been trying to kill all the prophets, especially me."

Elias stopped talking for a moment and a thoughtful look accentuated his face.

Sensing Elias had something to tell him, Adam asked, "Elias, what did you do now?"

He chuckled nervously. "I prophesied that Zelbe and Joab were going to be killed soon in a violent death."

"Really," Adam said, looking off in the distance. He spotted Aza and his soldiers hiding in the trees. He pointed in their direction to make sure Elias saw them. Hopefully, they weren't going to try anything at the wedding.

"You told them that?" Adam added. "I'm sure that went over well."

"I have to say what God tells me to say," Elias said. His gaze was fixed on Aza and his men. His whole body was tense.

Adam intended to hold him back if he made a move in that direction. Now was not the time for a confrontation. He did consider taking out his gun and firing a shot above their heads but thought better of it. No reason to startle the guests who had started to arrive. Elias probably needed to go back inside and greet them.

"So far, I've been safe from her," Elias added. "She's afraid to touch me, probably because of you."

"I hope your prophecy comes to pass and they both die."

"It will. Everything God says comes to pass. God punishes those who disobey him so blatantly."

Like the one who ate the apple in the garden.

Adam had wondered for years when God was going to punish him. Although, the guilt and shame might be punishment enough.

Elias never point-blank asked Adam if he was the one who ate the apple. Adam couldn't bring himself to tell him. He was too ashamed.

Neither of them said anything for a good minute. Both stared off in the distance at the soldiers.

"God's doing many great things." Elias had interrupted the silence with an encouraging tone. "We have to trust him, Adam. We don't know what God is doing through all of these troubles."

"I hope you're right. It seems like God has abandoned us."

"He hasn't. At the right time, he'll do something. You watch. It'll be when we least expect it."

Adam wasn't redeemable. He prayed every day that God would have mercy on the people of Adon. This wasn't their fault. He had begged God to let the punishment fall on him and not the people.

"I hope it's soon," Adam said, barely above a whisper.

A smile returned to Elias' face. "Enough with the serious talk. Be of good cheer, my brother. We're having a wedding. Today's a day to celebrate."

"I agree. This day should be about Benjamin."

"I think Sophie's more excited than Benjamin. He's our youngest. He's her baby. The last one to get married."

"So, you're going to be an empty nester?"

Elias had a puzzled look on his face. "What do you mean an *empty nester*?"

Adam laughed. "That's an expression from back on Earth. That's when all your kids leave the house. Like a bird whose little babies all finally leave the nest and fly away."

"I like that saying. What was that other one you always say that I like?"

"A piece of cake."

"That's the one. I remember the first time you said that. No idea what you meant."

"It means that things are going to be easy."

"I don't think things are going to be easy for any of us."

Adam changed the subject.

"Cake. I could use some cake," he said. "Your wife makes the best cake I've ever eaten. Did she make one for the wedding?"

"She did. Let's go inside and see if she needs anything. Let's get this party started."

Adam glanced back across the field. Aza and his soldiers weren't there anymore.

The conversation still rattled around in his mind. He wished he could believe things were going to be a piece of cake. That God was going to do something.

What could he do?

What would he do?

Adam had a gnawing feeling in the pit of his stomach that things were going to get much worse before they got better.

* * *

Elias and Sophie were beloved, and hundreds of people came from miles to celebrate the wedding.

Adam wondered how they were able to feed so many people. He had planted some of his seeds and made a garden. The area was hidden about a mile from his spacecraft, and no one knew it was there. He often brought food to Elias and his family. He had given them some a few days before as a wedding gift.

Most people were poor, including Elias and Sophie. King Joab and Zelbe had imposed an arduous tax on the people and used their soldiers to collect the tax. They hired hundreds of tax collectors who went around Adon forcing the people to pay it by the sharp edge of a sword.

They often took more than required and kept the money for themselves. No one had extra money for a wedding. No one had extra money for any luxuries. They were all barely surviving.

Not everyone lived poorly. King Joab and Queen Zelbe and all their elite friends were getting rich off the backs of the people of Adon. They built lush palaces and spared no expense to have the finest food and wine. They had servants at their beck and call to cater to their every need. Those things cost money, and the people were the ones who suffered so they could live in luxury.

Adam had asked Elias how he could afford a wedding with that many people. Elias simply said, "God will provide."

The guests brought food and presents to the extent that they could. Elias said he would provide the wine if his friends would bring enough food for themselves and one other person. They didn't send out specific invitations, they just let everyone know by word of mouth. Elias had no idea that so many people would show up.

Wine was in short supply, and Elias didn't have nearly enough.

Elias asked Adam to go out and see if he could find more. Adam went from house to house, offering to trade food for wine. He found some but not nearly enough. When he got back to the wedding reception, Adam had to give Elias the news that he only found a couple of pitchers of wine.

"Everyone has the same problem," Adam said. "They're all out of wine. There were some terrible storms over in the eastern district where they grow the grapes, and a lot of crops were destroyed. I have some grapes in my garden, but I didn't know that you'd need them. I could have made some wine, but of course, now it's too late."

"Don't worry about it, my friend. We will serve wine first and then water when it's all gone."

The house was packed with people milling around on the inside and outside.

"Come on Adam, I want to introduce you to someone I don't think you've met," Elias said.

They walked across the room toward a man standing with his back to them. A group of people were gathered around him.

Elias touched the man's shoulder, and he turned around to face them.

"Adam, I want you to meet someone," Elias said.

Adam knew immediately who it was.

"His name is Jesus," Elias said.

Adam's knees buckled. He would've fallen had Jesus not held him up.

4

Aza threw a party for his dad, King Joab, the same night as Elias' son's wedding. Dozens of guests had just left, and Aza and King Joab were being entertained privately by Aza's sisters who were forced to dance provocatively for their brother and dad as a gift from Aza.

The king said he was pleased with his son and told him he could choose any of the king's maid servants and take her back to his room when they were done.

Aza could hardly wait. It'd been a trying day. Chasing rebels across the countryside. Running into Adam, the Earthling. Following him to Elias' house where a large crowd had gathered.

He had watched for a while but eventually had to rush back for the birthday party.

"First, we need to take care of business," the king said, surprising Aza.

Aza had too much wine and wasn't interested in talking about anything other than going to bed with one of those young girls. He already had one in mind.

"What kind of business?" he asked.

The king clapped his hands and the girls stopped dancing and started to leave the room.

"Don't leave!" the king shouted in a roaring voice. "You girls keep dancing until I tell you to stop."

They looked frightened and confused. Huddled together, not sure what to do.

"Over there," the king said roughly. Pointing to a far corner of the room. "Dance over there."

The business must be important if the king wanted the girls out of earshot.

The king motioned to a servant to pour him and Aza some wine then instructed him to leave the room as well.

The girls were over in the corner. Talking among themselves.

"Dance!" the king shouted.

They started dancing slowly. Without much energy. They looked tired. They'd been pawed on for more than an hour by the two men and their guests.

The king didn't press the issue.

Aza might reprimand his sisters later that night, if he had the energy and the king didn't beat him to it. Maybe he'd wait until tomorrow.

"Where is the queen tonight?" Aza asked.

"I don't know, and I don't care. Probably off somewhere with her lover, Tristan. As long as she's nowhere near me, I'm happy." The king said it with a belly laugh.

Since the end of the Garden of Eden, the king had gained at least two hundred pounds.

Aza joined in the laughter. He didn't care much for his mother either.

"What kind of business do you want to discuss?" Aza asked.

"What have you heard about this so-called Messiah?" King Joab said with a scowl.

"I haven't heard much." Aza was reclined on a long lounge chair with his head propped up by one arm. Staring at the girls, who were barely dancing at all. He scowled at them, but it didn't have the same effect as it did when his father did it.

That'd change when he was king.

Aza continued. "I've heard the rumors. Probably the same thing you heard. One of the prophets said a Messiah is coming."

Eve had first mentioned it thirty years before. Right before she was killed. So far, nothing had come of it.

"Did they say when and where?"

Aza shook his head.

"The only thing I heard is that he comes from the east."

"We should kill all the newborn male children," Joab said. "Until the threat is gone. First born sons. If this Messiah has designs on being king, then he'll be a first-born son. The people wouldn't accept anything less."

"According to the prophets, he's already been born."

"How is that possible?"

"Do you remember the star from the east that was in the sky for nearly two years?"

The king took a big swig of his wine and grunted an affirmative answer.

"That's supposed to be a sign that the Messiah is coming."

"Then we'll kill all male children under say twelve."

"What if he was born when the star came?"

"That was thirty years ago."

"That's what I'm saying."

"Then let's kill all the men under thirty."

That sounded like a lot of work. The job would fall on him.

"I say it's easier to kill him after he reveals himself, and we know who he is."

The king scowled. Not particularly pleased with that solution but didn't offer an alternative. Thankfully. All the security of the king's reign already fell on Aza. He didn't want any more responsibility.

"Keep your eye out for anyone suspicious."

That reminded him.

"I saw a man go into Elias' house this afternoon. Someone I've never seen before."

"Tell me about this man."

"I asked around. Apparently, his name is Jesus. That's all I know."

"Is he under thirty?"

"Like I said, I've never seen him before. I don't know how old he is, but I can find out."

The king rubbed the whiskers of his beard. Deep in thought. Aza yawned. If they didn't finish the conversation soon, he might be too tired to have his way with the maid servant. An opportunity he didn't want to miss.

"A lot of people were at Elias' house," Aza said, knowing it'd get a rile out of the king.

"What were they doing there?"

"From what I could gather, someone was getting married."

"And this Jesus was there?"

"Yes. When he arrived, he had a huge following with him. They seemed enthralled by him."

"I have a bad feeling about this guy. We need to follow him. If Jesus was with Elias, then he's up to no good."

Aza didn't know where to begin looking for the man. If he'd known, he could've left one of his men to follow Jesus from the party.

He wanted to change the subject to the bigger threats.

"I saw Adam, the Earthling, at the party as well."

"That's strange. He doesn't usually leave his spacecraft. I wonder if he was there to see this Jesus character."

"I think he was there for the wedding. Elias is one of his closest friends."

Joab took another drink from his chalice before continuing. "Elias is the one I'm most worried about. Do you know what that vermin said in the temple yesterday?"

Aza didn't respond.

"Elias said that marrying Mena is an abomination to the Lord."

Joab threw his wooden chalice across the room at the girls, startling them. They had stopped dancing completely. The king glared at them, and they started back up.

Mena was the wife of Joab's brother. Who the king had killed for insurrection. The real reason Joab killed his brother was because he wanted to marry his wife who was strikingly beautiful.

"What business is it of Elias? The queen doesn't care," Joab said, angrily.

"She doesn't care how many wives you have, as long as you keep your power and share it with her."

"I don't care what your mother does either, as long as she leaves me alone and I rarely see her."

Aza nodded. "I won't rest until Adam is dead."

His hatred ran as deep as a knife plunged into a piece of meat. He despised the man.

"I want Elias dead." The king said it so matter-of-factly, it startled Aza for a moment.

"Elias is loved by the people. We must be careful when we go after him. We don't want a revolt."

"The people are weak. They don't have the will to revolt. Your soldiers will crush them."

"Adam's the one I think is the biggest danger."

Adam's threatening words from earlier that afternoon still rattled around in his brain. As did that feeling of fear he felt when Adam pulled his gun.

"Why don't you kill Adam?"

"You know I've tried. He has those weapons that fire projectiles. They kill people instantly."

"Maybe there's another way to hurt Adam. By hurting Elias."

"I think Adam's the one who ate the apple, but I can't prove it," Aza said.

Aza wanted to kill Elias, but he wanted to kill Adam more. Each were pushing their own agenda. The king would ultimately win out.

Although Aza was the one tasked with carrying it out. He didn't see a way to kill either of them at the moment.

"Someone knows who ate the apple," Aza said.

"If Adam ate it, then Elias would know. He and Adam are as thick as robbers. Let's offer a reward for information leading to the arrest of the one who ate the apple. Hopefully, someone will come forward with information about Adam, and then we can kill him."

"Seems like God is protecting him."

"God won't say anything if we prove Adam's the one who ate the apple."

That made sense. A reward. He hadn't thought of that. It wouldn't be hard to pay someone to make the accusation. If no one came forward.

"That's a good idea. I'll get right on it."

"Go after Elias. See what he knows. Arrest him and torture him until he breaks. If he won't talk, have him stoned to death in front of all the people. We need to make an example of him. That might deter this Messiah from showing his face."

"I'll do that tomorrow," Aza said with a wide grin. "First, I'm going to find that young servant girl with the blonde hair."

He'd been waiting to fit that into the conversation.

"A good choice. She's only fifteen and still a virgin."

The king called for one of the sisters to go and get his servant. When the man returned, the king had him retrieve his chalice, fill it with wine, then go find the young girl and bring her back there.

Aza and the king drank for several minutes. The palace guard flung open the door and led the girl into the room with a strong grip on her wrist.

Aza stood and walked over to her.

She was shivering.

He put his arm around her.

She instinctively pulled away.

He grabbed her by the arm.

She let out a weak scream.

Aza slapped the girl across her face. She tried to run away but he was too strong. He picked her up over his shoulder and carried her out of the room kicking and screaming. The screams echoed through the entire palace.

5

Jesus looked nothing like Adam had pictured in his mind and even less like the pictures he'd seen back on earth.

Slight build, scraggly beard, and a crook in his nose accented his forgettable features. Dark brown, shoulder length hair was well kept. His robe was understated but functional.

Jesus still gripped his hand even though Adam had regained his footing. The shock of seeing the Son of God had sent Adam's head spinning.

Jesus pulled Adam toward him and kissed him on the cheek.

"I already know Adam," Jesus said.

"Sorry," Elias said. "I didn't realize you two had met."

Jesus' eyes were penetrating. Deep into Adam's soul. Adam looked away. Then back again. His gaze was drawn toward the man.

Then a rush of doubt flooded his mind. His skeptical nature kicked in. Maybe this wasn't the Jesus of the Bible. A lot of people on Adon could be named Jesus. Adam hadn't met any. That didn't mean they didn't exist.

After a whirlwind of arguments filled his mind, he had convinced himself this wasn't the Christ.

But why did he say he knew me?

They'd never met.

Jesus of the Bible did know him. Had known him since before the foundation of the worlds. According to the Bible.

Did the same thing apply to Adon?

Adam studied the man standing before him closely.

It can't be him.

He didn't have the look. He seemed like any other man. His hands were rough.

"Jesus is a skilled craftsman," Elias said. "A carpenter by trade."

Adam's heart skipped a beat. The Earthly Jesus was a carpenter.

Jesus smiled.

While his look wasn't what Adam expected, his manner and tone were. His voice was gentle and easy to listen to, pleasing to the ears. Loving eyes were matched by a caring and gentle touch.

Adam searched those eyes for any hint of judgment. He found none.

Before anyone had a chance to say anything else, Jesus was swept away by a throng of people who wanted to talk to him.

Adam was left stunned. Trying to process this new development.

It could only mean one thing.

If he really was the son of God, then God had sent him to Adon to be a sacrifice for Adam's sin.

* * *

The wedding ceremony was festive. The food was plentiful. Adam wondered if Jesus had multiplied the food or if the people had simply brought that much.

Adam didn't enjoy it. He barely noticed. A debate raged in his mind. He kept going back and forth.

He is the Christ. No! He isn't.

Adam avoided Jesus. Kept a safe distance.

Either way, the guilt flowed through him like water through a broken dam. That's what he felt like inside. Broken. Ashamed.

Did God intend to take all of the punishment he deserved and put it on this man?

Adam had read the Bible more times than he could count. Hundreds of times in space and dozens of times over the last thirty years. It was the only thing that brought him comfort.

Especially the gospels. He'd read over and over again how Jesus came to earth to die for man's sins. Through Christ every sin on earth was forgiven.

The words were only print on paper. They seemed so real now. The thought of meeting the real Jesus was more than he could comprehend.

He'd read about the crucifixion. The scourging. What Jesus suffered because of Adam's sin on earth.

Was history repeating itself on Adon?

It made sense.

Jesus came to earth because man needed a savior.

Adon needed a savior now. All because of him. Was Jesus forced to come there because of what Adam did?

Unimaginable.

How could he live with himself? He wanted to go back to the spacecraft and end his life.

He'd had the same thought over the years. He hadn't killed himself because on the other side was eternal judgment. Hell.

As bad as things were on Adon, hell was worse.

And he had found a purpose. A reason to stay alive. To protect Elias and his family from Joab, Aza, and the Queen.

Adam was offered wine. He avoided it. He wanted to keep his wits about him. To think clearly. He also knew they were running short of wine. Sophie seemed beside herself. She wanted everything to be perfect for her son's wedding. Adam felt a mountain of guilt and blamed himself for that problem.

God provided all the food and wine to the people before the fall. Everyone had more than enough. Food, water, clothing, and shelter. All of which were now in short supply.

Avoiding Jesus was no longer possible. Their eyes met. Jesus walked toward him.

"Adam, I'd like to talk to you alone," he said. "Outside. Away from the people."

Adam's heart was racing. Doing laps around his chest. Beating so hard, Adam could hear it in his ears.

Maria, Jesus's mother, approached and interrupted them. Before either could move toward the door.

"Jesus, Elias has run out of wine," she said.

"How's that my problem? My time has not yet come." [1]

The words sounded eerily familiar. He remembered that same conversation in the Bible.

It didn't sound to Adam like Jesus was saying it with disrespect or defiance. It sounded more like he was just stating a fact.

Elias had a group of workers helping serve the guests at the wedding. Maria motioned for them to come to her. The determined look on her face signified she was going to take charge like only a mother could.

"Do whatever he tells you," she said, pointing at Jesus.

Maria then looked at Jesus with a stern look as if to say, *I'm your mother. I want you to take care of this problem.*

Adam smiled at the exchange, wondering if what was coming was the same as what he had read about in the Bible.

Jesus's first miracle on earth was turning water into wine.

At a wedding!

Adam welcomed the interruption. Jesus had wanted to go outside and talk. Adam dreaded the conversation.

He followed Jesus to the other room. Anticipating what was about to happen.

This would prove it. If this really was the same Jesus, he would turn the water into wine.

Adam was torn. On the one hand, he wanted it to be the Christ. On the other hand, he didn't want to face the judgment. To look the real Jesus in the eye and explain why he ate the apple. Knowing the consequences would bring sin and death to Adon.

Standing near the front door were seven water jars. The purpose was for guests to use them to wash themselves when they arrived. Each of the water pots held twenty to thirty gallons of water. They were empty because water was in short supply. Elias hadn't even bothered to fill them.

Jesus told the workers, "Fill the jars with water."

The workers didn't immediately react.

'You would use up your entire water supply if we did that," one of them said.

"That's okay," Elias said. "Just do what he says."

When the jars were filled, Jesus said, "Now dip some out, and take it to one of the guests."

They followed his instructions.

When the man tasted the water, it wasn't water, but wine. He called Benjamin, the groom over and said, "You've been holding out on us. Normally, a groom serves the best wine first. After we've all had a lot to drink, we won't notice the less expensive wine. You saved the best for last."

The water was turned into wine!

It is him!

The crowd roared in approval. Adam smiled at the irony or perhaps God's plan.

He had his confirmation.

This was the Christ.

An overwhelming joy flooded his soul. Surprisingly. The guilt and shame tried to offset it but couldn't.

Adam wanted to have that conversation now. Curiosity flowed through him. Maybe it was the scientist in him. The one who liked to know things. He had talked to God in the garden. The thought of actually talking to Jesus was exhilarating.

He kept looking for an opportunity. None came for several hours.

The water jars continued to be filled until everyone had had enough to drink. Every time the servers went back to the water barrels, they found them full. After everyone had enough to drink, more wine was left over.

Everyone was amazed at the miracle. The people didn't want to leave. They stayed well into the night.

Eventually the crowd was gone and Adam helped clean up. By that time, he had lost his courage. He wanted to leave with them, but Elias insisted he spend the night. Too dangerous to walk back to the spacecraft.

Jesus was still there. The crowd had demanded his full attention. Everyone knew Jesus had performed a miracle in their midst.

Of course, they didn't know what Adam knew.

Adam mustered up the courage to approach him. "Can we talk now?" he asked. "Outside. Alone."

Jesus followed Adam outside. The area was behind the house. The outside was dimly lit.

Hesitant at first, Adam finally spoke. "Are you the same Jesus who's in the Bible?"

"Who do you say I am?" Jesus replied.

"I think you are the Christ."

Jesus got a serious look on his face. "Adam, you're not to tell anyone who I am. I must suffer many things, but no one is to know until I tell them."

Adam shook his head no, emphatically. "I know why you came to Adon. It's all because of me."

He spoke urgently but barely above a whisper. "I'm the one who ate the apple. It's not fair for you to suffer because of me. I'm the one who should be killed, not you."

"Adam, all have sinned and fall short of the glory of God,"[2] Jesus said lovingly.

"They didn't sin until I did what I did. Why are they being punished for my sin? Why do you have to die for what I did?"

Adam tried to continue, but Jesus interrupted him.

"Adam, they didn't eat the apple, but they've all sinned and have sin in their hearts. No one can come to the Father but through me. If I don't die, they cannot be saved."

"I should be the one who dies, not you. They're going to kill you because of me."

Adam could imagine Joab and Aza being the ones to seize Jesus and kill him.

He wasn't going to let that happen.

"I give my life freely,"[3] Jesus said. "No one takes it from me. What I do is because it is the will of the Father. Don't concern yourself with that. Come with me, Adam. Help me preach the good news. The harvest is plentiful, but the workers are few."

Adam's shoulders sagged. "I can't do that. I'm not worthy. You know what I've done. No way God can use me."

"Adam, where are your accusers?"[4] Jesus looked around.

Adam didn't respond.

"I don't accuse you, either. Go and sin no more and follow me."

He looked at Adam with such compassion, Adam believed him. Not all the guilt and shame were gone, but a resolve rose up inside of him to follow Christ even to the point of death.

"Do you remember what Elias said when he first met you?" Jesus asked.

How did he know about Elias and what he said?

"He said God has a plan for you. Adam, listen to me carefully. God wants to use you to save the people."

Adam couldn't contain his amazement. The meaning of the words hit him between the eyes. More confirmation he was the all-knowing Christ.

"God wants to use *me*? Why? How?"

"The time has not yet come for you to know. There'll be a moment someday when God is going to use you. Be prepared for that time," Jesus said.

"I can't believe God would want to use me. After all I've done."

"Meet me at Mount Shalam in two days. Bring nothing with you—no bag, no food, no money, no extra shirt. Only bring seven food packets with you. Five bread and two fish."

"Okay. I'll meet you."

"Leave your gun behind," Jesus said. "You won't need it. Trust God."

Adam started to say he didn't have a gun but stopped himself. Jesus obviously already knew he had a gun, or he wouldn't have said anything.

"Two days. Mount Shalam. I'll be there," Adam said.

Jesus disappeared into the night.

6

The next day

Adam barely slept. He spent most of the day preparing to leave the spacecraft and meet Jesus at Mount Shalam.

A number of conflicting thoughts swirled around in his head.

How could he leave everything to follow Jesus? His food. Shelter. Weapons. Jesus emphatically said to only bring five loaves of bread and two fish.

And to leave his gun behind. That felt like insanity.

What about Aza? Joab? The soldiers?

Even getting to Mount Shalam without his gun as protection was no guarantee. Jesus said he'd protect him. Could Adam trust that?

A horrific thought entered his head. What if the man he met the night before wasn't really Jesus? What if he was an imposter?

Elias seemed to vouch for him. How well did Elias know him?

They could be blindly following a charlatan.

It seemed like such a foolish thought. Adam kept beating himself up for having doubts.

The man's name was Jesus. That should be proof enough. He basically came right out and said he was the Christ. Privately anyway. Jesus had admonished him not to tell anyone.

It was all he could do to keep from telling Elias after Jesus left. Especially when he started talking about a coming Messiah. Adam bit his lip and kept quiet.

He couldn't stop the thoughts from entering his head. What if the man pretended to be the Jesus in the Bible?

Who else on Adon knew about the biblical accounts? Adam racked his brain trying to remember. He definitely told Elias. Even showed him a Bible. He told Adam and Eve. Maybe. He couldn't remember for sure.

Elias could've told someone else. Probably did. He would've certainly told Sophia. His sons. Other prophets.

With all the talk of a Messiah, a common man might've heard the rumors and seized the opportunity. Several false prophets on earth pretended to be a savior. Some even claimed to be a modern-day Jesus.

A horrifying thought caused Adam to stop what he was doing.

What if the man was sent there by Aza? As a trap, to separate Adam from his weapons.

An anger rose up inside of him as he convinced himself of it. At least momentarily.

Common sense eventually took over.

I saw Jesus turn water into wine.

A cheap magician's trick.

His skeptical mind was coming up with rebuttals as fast as he could make the arguments.

He told me things about me that only the Son of God would know.

Lucky guess.

No!

It had to be him. Adam tried to fight back the negative thoughts, but confusion raged inside of him.

Nevertheless, he kept preparing to leave. His thoughts turned to not burning bridges in case he had to return to the spacecraft.

Maybe he should save some of his food.

Take a gun with him.

Jesus said not to. Would that make Jesus angry? So much so that he wouldn't let Adam go with him?

He couldn't take the risk. He had to do what Jesus said to do.

Was he supposed to simply follow Jesus with blind faith?

Wasn't that what following Christ was like on Earth? Believing in Jesus even though they hadn't seen him in the flesh. That's why Adam had been an atheist. None of it made sense to his educated and analytical mind.

Eventually, to appease Courtney, he had switched to labeling himself an agnostic, meaning he simply didn't know if God existed.

Well, now he knew. He had seen God in the garden. Talked to him. God had miraculously healed his burns.

Now he had met Jesus. He was certain of it.

The Bible said blessed was the man who has not seen and yet believed.[1]

Adam felt guilty. He'd seen Jesus and had less faith than Courtney and his daughter Jamie who had never seen him.

He should be excited. How many people in the universe ever got this opportunity?

But how did he know the same scenario in the Bible would play out on Adon?

He didn't. But he had to find out. He had no choice but to go down this path. Wherever it led.

What was he going to do with all this food?

His garden was ready for harvest. It seemed like a shame to waste it. He had enough provision to feed dozens of families for a year or so. He had enough seeds to feed himself for hundreds of years.

The doubts returned. Was he really going to leave all this behind? On blind faith.

What difference does it make?

Since the fall, Adam had noticed something. He was aging. While he was in space, he barely aged at all. Over the last thirty years, he could tell he was growing older. Not as fast as on Earth, but faster than before.

He'd never live long enough to eat all the food his spacecraft would provide.

Didn't want to, anyway. His was a miserable existence. Whatever fate awaited him following Jesus, couldn't be any worse than the future he faced now.

Don't be so sure.

Those who followed Jesus in the Bible faced tremendous hardship and suffering.

He came up with a plan. He'd harvest the food and take it to Adon. Give to the needy. Jesus would certainly approve of that sentiment.

It took several trips, but he hauled all the food from his garden over to the city and left it on a corner. Word spread quickly and a crowd gathered. When he arrived carrying the last load, things had escalated into a near riot.

Not what Adam had intended. People were fighting over the provisions.

The strongest overpowered the weak. Women and children tried to press in and get some food, but the men pushed them aside. If any of them did manage to grab anything, it was quickly ripped out of their hands.

Adam was helpless to stop them. He tried to help a few people, but he was putting himself at risk. A lot of the food was being wasted as it fell to the ground. Maybe the women and children could get some of the crumbs.

He hurried back to the spacecraft with tears rolling down his cheeks.

Blaming himself.

Was he always going to feel this way?

Was he to blame for every single bad thing that happened on Adon? Didn't those people who had no regard for their fellow human beings hold some responsibility for their behaviors? Pushing little children aside just because they could. Hoarding the provisions, leaving others starving because of their own greed.

Maybe that's what Jesus meant by all have sinned. On earth, the first man, Adam, brought sin into the world by eating the apple. But that's no excuse for all the ones who came after. They chose to sin as well. Including him.

Wouldn't the same thing be true on Adon?

He certainly had his own sins to account for. On Earth and on Adon. He was paying the price for both. These people who behaved badly would have to answer to God for their own sins regardless of who brought sin into the world.

At some point, he had to let it go. He couldn't carry the burden for every citizen of Adon. What happened, happened. Nothing he could do about it now.

Other than try and do some good. Which was why he spent so much effort to get food to the people.

Jesus was giving him a new opportunity. One he needed to focus on. Adam didn't know what that entailed, but he was excited again. A nervous anticipation overrode how tired he felt.

After a long day, he fell into bed exhausted. Even then, he had to force himself to close his eyes and get some sleep.

The next morning, he secured the spacecraft and was ready to go. The plan was for him to go to Elias' house and walk with him to meet Jesus.

Adam looked around Chronos with a sense of sadness. He'd spent three hundred years of his life on that vessel, and while he wouldn't necessarily miss it, it had a special place in his heart.

Chronos brought him to Adon where he met God and Jesus.

He looked at himself in the mirror with a great deal of satisfaction. A new adventure awaited him. Jesus had chosen him, and Adam was thrilled.

The doubts were gone. If not gone, then locked in the deep recesses of his mind. If Jesus was an imposter, he'd soon know it.

He locked up the spacecraft, wondering if he'd ever be back there again. Satisfied he took care of every detail, Adam headed off to Elias' house with only the clothes on his back and the seven packets of food as Jesus had commanded.

He came into the city. The food was gone when he passed the corner, and he forced a smile to his face. Hopefully, the food would be helpful to somebody deserving.

Adam had to slow his step. The excitement and anticipation of walking with Jesus was invigorating.

If Courtney could see me now.

He rounded a corner and stopped in his tracks. Ahead were nine of Aza's soldiers congregating along the side of the road. Adam started walking with a purpose, hoping they wouldn't notice him, or if they did, would leave him alone.

As he neared them, four stepped off the side of the road, directly into his path, blocking it. The other five circled around behind him.

Instinctively, Adam reached for his gun, forgetting Jesus had told him to leave it behind. Fear set in as he wasn't sure what to do. Jesus had said to trust God, and that's what he would have to do.

Apparently, reaching for the gun was enough to get their attention because the four in the front parted like the Red Sea and Adam quickly made his way through them.

When the men were out of sight, Adam finally allowed himself to relax and take a deep breath. As he did, a young boy, who Adam didn't know, came running up to him.

"Elias . . ." the boy said, trying to catch his breath. "Elias has been arrested."

"When did that happen?"

"The soldiers came to his house this morning and took him away. He's in the prison just ahead. His wife told me to find you and tell you."

"What's his wife's name?" Adam asked, not fully believing the boy.

The boy took off running without giving Adam another chance to respond.

Who was that boy? Was this a trap?

He wasn't sure what to do. If they had Elias, he had no choice but to try and help him. He left the main road and took side roads to the prison, trying to stay out of the sight of any other soldiers.

He found a place to hide near the prison where he could watch the entrance but not be seen. Very few people were going in and out. The main entrance didn't seem to be guarded.

Why wouldn't guards be posted?

It smelled like a trap. It didn't matter. He had to go in. Elias was his friend and would do the same for him.

Adam waited until no one was watching and ran to the steps of the prison and through the door. As he had observed, no one was guarding the main entrance. The prison was really more a series of caves. The entrance had a place for the guards to stand and steps led down to the depths of the caves.

Children often played there before the fall.

Adam blinked several times, trying to adjust his eyes to the darkness. Torches provided some light but barely enough to keep from running into anything. He made his way down the stairs. Elias wasn't in any of the cells on the first or second level.

When he got to the third level, deep inside the caves, Adam called out for Elias, barely able to make out anything in the darkness.

"Elias. Are you here?" Adam said quietly not wanting to attract the attention of a guard.

"Adam, is that you?" Elias said in a weak voice.

He is here!

"I'm coming. I'm going to get you out of here."

The door to Elias's cell was open.

Something doesn't seem right.

Adam looked around and then walked inside. In the back corner of the cell, Elias was bound with his hands and head in stocks. Chains were wrapped around his feet and attached to the wall. Open wounds from a beating formed a puddle of blood at his feet.

"My good friend," Elias said. "Looks like I'm the one who needs healing now."

Adam didn't know how to lay hands on Elias and see him healed.

"I'm going to get you out of here," Adam said, as he tried to figure out how to get his friend out of the stocks.

Elias managed a grin.

Movement.

Behind him.

Someone was hiding in the shadows. Adam lunged for the cell door but too late to stop it from closing.

Aza! It was a trap.

7

That same morning

I spent the night at Mount Shalam praying and the morning waiting for my twelve disciples to arrive—the twelve whom I had chosen as was my custom. That number was significant to God and to me as well.

Twelve meant perfection and authority.

They would be responsible for carrying on my work when I'm gone. I always chose unremarkable men by the planet's standards. God uses the foolish things of the world to confound the wise.[1] I didn't choose the best looking, the richest, best educated, or the most talented. I chose men who everyone would know could not do the great things on their own.

That way, my Father got the glory for the things they did, not them.

Adon was the last world. These disciples would be the last. My work would finally be over. I thought back over all the worlds with great affection, Mars, Jupiter, Venus, Saturn, Mercury, Pluto, Uranus, Neptune, Earth, Adon and all the others. I remember them like they were my own children, which they were.

Not all the disciples had remained faithful to the end. Some had betrayed me; some had denied me.

I still loved them.

Adon, being the last world, compelled me to reflect back on the history of all the worlds. I remember the conversation before any of the planets existed, before man was ever created.

I remember it like it was yesterday. My Father, the Holy Spirit, and I had talked about the possibility of creating worlds for many eons. My Father first came up with the idea.

"We can take the particles of the universe and make them into solar systems," God had said. "Each solar system will have planets that circle a light source."

"For what purpose?" I asked.

"To make man to inhabit them. Male and female."

"What is man?"

"We will make man in our own image to live in the worlds and have dominion and authority over them. It's not good for us to be alone, and man will give us companionship in heaven for an eternity. We'll have a throng of worshipers."

God described man to us in great detail.

"Will man have free will?" I asked.

"Yes. He must have free will. He must be free to choose his own destiny," God said.

I agreed. We always agreed. "It wouldn't be true worship, if man didn't have the right to want to worship us."

"The evil one will try to turn him away from us," the Holy Spirit said.

Many years before, Satan had rebelled against God, and a great battle ensued. As a result, God cast Satan and a third of the angels out of heaven. God and Satan had been warring ever since.

The final battle would be coming soon.

"What if man sins like the evil one and rebels against you?" I asked.

"He will. I have foreseen it."

God had been right. On every planet in every solar system was a garden of Eden. An Adam and an Eve. A tree of the knowledge of good and evil.

Man had always rebelled against God. Eaten the forbidden fruit.

Adon was no different. Even though Adam was from Earth, one of their own, Aza, would've eventually sinned. The evil one would've tricked him. Only a matter of time. To their credit, they held out longer than the others.

My mind wandered back to the conversation before the foundations of the worlds.

"I already love man," I had said.

I had a picture of man in my mind. What God intended. A being with flesh and blood in a body. With a soul and spirit. With emotions. The ability to love like we loved.

Brilliant.

The plan had its risks. It'd break my heart if man ended up like Satan and a third of the angels. God would never allow man in heaven with us for an eternity if he sinned against him.

I voiced my concern.

"If man sins, he'll not be able to live in heaven with us for an eternity," I said.

"There must be a sacrifice for those sins in order for them to get into heaven," God said.

"What kind of sacrifice?"

"The sacrifice must be perfect and must die."

"I will be that sacrifice," I said emphatically.

"How can you die, unless you become like them?" the Holy Spirit asked. "You are immortal."

"I could go to the different worlds, as a man. I could live among them."

"You can't sin. God said the sacrifice had to be perfect."

"I'll face the same temptations and overcome them on their behalf so the sacrifice will be perfect."

"You can't possess a man's body," the Holy Spirit said.

"He can be born of a virgin," God explained. "Fully man, but also fully God."

"Interesting," the Holy Spirit said.

"What will I do once I go to the planets?" I asked.

"You will have to suffer many great things," God said.

"Like what?"

"Without the shedding of blood, there can be no remission of sin."[2]

"I must shed my blood?"

"Yes."

"I am willing."

"You must take on their sins."

"I will bear their sins."

"Their sins create sickness and disease."

"I will bear their sicknesses and diseases."

"Their sins create great sorrows."

"I will bear their sorrows."

"The judgment of them all will be upon you."

"I will take their judgment. Their punishment shall be on me."

"They will feel shame."

"I will take their shame upon myself."

"I will not be able to look upon you."

"You would forsake me?"

"Yes."

"I don't know if I could bear that."

"I cannot look upon sin. Even if it's on my own son."

"I can't be separated from you for an eternity."

"Not for an eternity. For three days you will go to hell. Set free a host of captives. On the third day, I will raise you up in a new body. Then you will be delivered into the heavens and be seated at my right hand. Making intercession for man."

"I am willing."

"Then it shall be done."

"Thy will be done. On the planets as it is in heaven."

"Then all of my riches of the universe will be yours," God said.

"All I ask is that you make man joint-heirs in those riches," I said.

"They must believe in you to be a joint-heir. They must believe that I have sent you. That you are my son."

"Of course. Why wouldn't they believe in me? I'll save them from their sins. Offer them eternal life."

"There is none righteous. No not one.[3] Many will reject you."

"I will lay down my life for them. No greater love has any man than to lay down his life.[4] Surely, they will all follow me."

"The road to destruction is broad. Narrow is the gate to enter into eternal life."[5]

"If I take their punishment, you cannot punish them."

"Whosoever believeth in you will not perish but have everlasting life."[6]

"They will be the righteousness of God in Christ," the Holy Spirit said.

"They will be holy because I am holy," Jesus replied. "When you look at them, you will see me. For they will be in me and I in them."

"I will punish them for an eternity if they don't believe in you. Justice demands it."

"How will you punish them?"

"They will be cast into the lake of fire."

"We created that for Satan and his demons. After he was thrown out of heaven."

"Man will perish there for rejecting you. I will reward those who believe in you."

"What must they do to be saved?"

"Confess with their mouth that you are Lord and believe that I have raised you from the dead and they shall be saved.[7] Then they will live for an eternity with us in heaven."

"I will prepare a place for each of them. I will build many mansions."

"On the planets, there will be much suffering. In heaven, there will be no tears. No sickness. No pain."

"Surely man will want to go to heaven."

"How will they hear without a preacher?"[8] the Holy Spirit asked.

"I will draw all men unto me," I said.

"They will be without excuse," God said.

"They will call upon me."

"How shall they call on him in whom they have not believed?" the Holy Spirit asked.

Jesus didn't answer.

"How shall they believe in him of whom they have not heard? And how shall they hear without a preacher?" the Holy Spirit added.

"I will write my laws on their hearts," God said. "All creation will reveal my invisible qualities. My eternal power and divine nature. They will clearly be able to see me and understand."

"I will raise up apostles, prophets, evangelists. Some as pastors, teachers. For the perfecting of the saints, for the work of the ministry," I said. "That's how they will hear."

"I will come upon them with power. I will give them gifts," the Holy Spirit exclaimed. "And fruit. Love. Joy. Peace. Patience. Kindness. Goodness. Gentleness. Self-Control. All the attributes that we possess."

"They will be born again. Made new creatures in me."

The ideas were flowing fast.

"I will protect them. Give them abundant life on the planets."

"You are my son. I'm pleased with you," God said.

"All that you give to me, give to them as well."

God agreed.

Then continued, "Your name will be Jesus, which means salvation. You will die for the people's sins, and then I will raise you from the dead three days later. You'll be seated at my right hand for an eternity."

"If I leave man and come to heaven, they will be alone to fight the enemy."

I turned to the Holy Spirit and asked him, "After I leave the planets, I want to send you to live inside of each believer. Will you go? You can empower them to overcome the evil one. I want to give them my peace. You can provide them everything they need while on their planet. I will tell you what to say to them."

"I am willing," the Holy Spirit said.

After all the details were decided on, God created what he called the *Lamb's Book of Life*. In the book, he wrote the name of every person who would ever live.

God knew them before they were created. Each one had a different fingerprint. If I were to ask, God could tell me how many hairs each of them had on their heads.

He was so creative. Had the idea for male and female. God came up with the idea for marriage. They'd become one flesh. Physically and spiritually. In different type of bodies. With different functions. They would be able to procreate. Create more men and women on their own so more could experience eternal life.

"There will be no marriage in heaven," God said.

We agreed that was a good idea.

When the *Lamb's Book of Life* was done, and all the names were written in it, God said, "These are our sons and our daughters. Whom I love. If they believe in my son, I will never erase their names from the book of life."

At the appointed time, God spoke the worlds into existence. On Earth, they called it a "Big Bang." That makes me chuckle. It was a big bang. God's words caused a huge explosion. Every particle in the universe was told where to go and what to do.

My heart was troubled. Thinking about man and his foolishness. Why couldn't they see that the creation had a creator.

So many had been lost. So many rejected me and God's plan. Billions of names had been blotted out of the book. Each name was a lost soul.

Why?

It had to be that way. It had to be their choice. I desired that no man would perish. So did God.

But he was righteous.

Soon the book would be sealed. The number of the elect chosen. When my work on Adon was over.

I had seen the end times.

God would cast all unbelievers into the lake of fire, and they'd perish. There'd be a great chasm between heaven and hell so that Satan and his demons could never reach us in heaven again.

Their fate would be an eternity of torment. They would never perish.

My thoughts were interrupted by one of my disciples.

I brushed away the tears.

"Ten of us are here. Two are missing," he said.

"I know. I must go and pray. Adam and Elias are still in grave danger."

8

Aza slammed the cell door and locked it before Adam had a chance to stop him, his taunts and laughter still resonated and echoed through the cave. The entire thing had been a carefully devised trap. Even the young boy was probably in on it.

Aza disappeared up the stairs.

Elias had been arrested earlier in the day and severely flogged and was already in the cell. His wounds needed medical attention. Adam tried to free him from the stocks, but they were fastened with chains.

Aza returned a couple of minutes later. He stood a few feet back from the cell door. Out of Adam's reach.

Adam regretted having left his gun at the spacecraft.

"Elias will be stoned to death tomorrow," Aza said. "You, Adam, will be left in this cell to rot. I will only give you enough food and water to keep you alive long enough so I can watch you suffer."

"God won't let you touch me," Adam retorted.

"Look, God," Aza said mockingly. "I'm not touching Adam. You never said I couldn't let him starve to death in a dungeon."

Aza laughed diabolically.

"Guard them carefully," he said to the jailer, then left.

Adam immediately turned to comforting Elias. He had been beaten nearly to death. Nothing Adam could do for his wounds.

Even in his weakness, Elias was in good spirits and happy to see his friend.

The jailer checked on them periodically and seemed to have compassion on them. Adam implored him to let them go, but he said Aza would take his life if he did so.

Adam became distraught. Not as much from the conditions but from the realization that he wouldn't be able to meet Jesus that morning. He'd looked forward to walking with Jesus. Aza took that from him.

The hatred for Aza was building in Adam.

If I could just get my hands on him.

Adam shook the cell bars, testing them for any weakness. He looked for any way of escape but found none. Then he devised a plan. When Aza and his men came for Elias the next morning, he would spring a trap and try to overpower them. The odds weren't great, but they were all he had.

I will not let them take Elias. I will not stay in this cell to die. Better to die fighting.

Elias believed God was going to deliver them from Aza's hand.

"Jesus told us to meet him at Mount Shalam. He wouldn't tell us to meet him if he knew there was no way we could. We must have faith in God," Elias said.

A thought came to Adam. A remembrance. Something he had read.

Paul and Silas. The jailer. Earthquake.

He quickly related the biblical account to Elias. Paul and Silas were in similar dire circumstances on Earth. Beaten with rods, they were thrown into a prison cell and bound in chains.

"They praised and worshiped God and were delivered by an earthquake right at midnight," Adam said excitedly.

"Hey jailer. What time is it?" Adam asked.

"It's ten o'clock."

"We can wait until midnight," Adam said. "We'll pray for God to deliver us then."

Elias let out a chuckle. "If we're going to believe God will deliver us at midnight, why not make it noon? Why wait twelve more hours? It takes faith either way."

"That's a good point. For the next two hours, let's praise and worship God, believing he will deliver us," Adam said.

He struggled to find faith to match the words. God might do this for Elias. But would he do it for Adam? After his horrible sin.

Elias must've sensed Adam's doubts. He said, "We walk by faith, not by sight."[1]

"Paul said that in the Bible."

"It's true. Faith is what we hope for. Not what we see. It's a confident expectation. We need to expect God to deliver us."

"It's hard when you don't see it."

"Speak what you want to have happen."

Adam spoke to the jailer, "At noon today, God is going to deliver us from these chains and this prison cell."

The jailer mocked them.

That emboldened Adam.

Adam and Elias ignored the taunts and started singing, making the loudest din throughout all the levels of the prison. They weren't the best singers. The jailer yelled for them to stop several times. But they ignored him and soon lost track of time as they immersed themselves in singing praises to God.

Without notice, the ground began to shake violently.

The cell door sprung open.

The stocks fell off Elias. Chains were released from his feet. His wounds were completely healed.

"What time is it?" Adam asked.

"It must be noon. God has delivered us."

Adam and Elias didn't immediately rush out of the cell. They grasped arms and jumped around, laughing, and dancing and celebrating what God had done for them.

Adam pulled Elias into a big hug. Then got a strange look on his face.

"What?" Elias said.

"Brother, you stink. God healed you of your wounds. He should've healed you from your smell."

They laughed heartily.

They made their way out of the cell and to the top of the stairs. Near the exit. The jailer was paralyzed in fear.

All of the prisoners in the cave were free. Their chains had fallen off of them as well and the doors to their cells opened. None had fled. They heard Adam and Elias praising God. About the prediction of a deliverance at noon. No doubt shocked when it happened.

They wanted to know more.

Adam and Elias shared with them how God had delivered them.

The jailer reached for his sword to take his own life. Adam stopped him.

"You don't have to take your life," Adam said.

"Don't harm yourself," Elias said. "We are all here."

"Aza will kill me. What must I do to be saved?" the jailer asked.

"Believe in the Lord Jesus, and you will be saved—you and your household," Adam said.

"Who is this Jesus?"

All the prisoners wanted to know.

"He is the Messiah who has come to take away the sins of Adon."

The jailer was filled with joy because he believed in God. He invited them to his house, but Adam told him they couldn't go.

"We have somewhere we have to be," Adam said looking at Elias with a wide grin.

"Mount Shalam," they said in unison.

"Go and gather your family," Elias said to the jailer. "They aren't safe at your house."

Elias told him where to go. Where his friends could hide him and his family.

"Tell them I sent you to them."

"I'm a jailer. They won't believe me."

"Tell them of the miraculous thing your eyes have seen. How the Lord delivered us from our chains."

"I will."

"Go quickly. Before someone comes."

The prisoners dispersed in several directions. Those who didn't have families followed Elias and Adam.

As they were walking, Adam turned to Elias and said, "I would love to be a fly on the wall in Aza's house."

Elias had a puzzled look on his face. "Why? I don't understand what you mean. Why would you want to be a fly?"

Adam laughed. "It's an expression, my friend. I would love to see Aza's reaction when he learns we're no longer there."

"Not me. I'm ready to get to Jesus. I hope they haven't left yet."

A horrible thought popped into Adam's head. If they had left, he had no idea where to go looking for them.

* * *

Aza was tired but pleased. He'd gotten up early that morning planning his revenge on Adam. His plan had worked to perfection. Adam and Elias, his two biggest threats, were in prison. Elias would be dead this time tomorrow and Adam would suffer a slow and agonizing death in the bowels of the prison.

He looked around his bedroom in the palace trying to keep his eyes open. Two women lay next to him. Wine stained the floor, clothes were strewn about, and furniture was turned over, providing evidence of the wild party that had just happened. Over the last two hours, before he fell into bed with exhaustion, they'd had all kinds of fun.

A brief smile went across his face as he remembered it. The two young girls had helped him celebrate his great victory. His father would be pleased. He hadn't had a chance to tell him yet.

He was almost asleep when the ground began to shake. Violently. Dishes on the tables fell to the ground making the loudest sounds. Parts of the stone on the walls and ceiling began to peel off and come crashing to the ground.

What was happening?

Aza had never seen the ground shake like that before.

The girls raised their heads.

One let out a scream.

Aza bolted out of bed. He tried to stand but lost his balance and fell to the ground from the undulations in the floor.

He could hear screaming outside of his bedroom door. People running. Why were they running? They should be coming to protect him.

As fast as the shaking had started, it stopped. He didn't move for several seconds while he waited to see what would happen next.

Guards appeared at his door to check on him. Aza instructed his captain of the guards to go and check on the prisoners.

Once the excitement died down, he climbed back into bed. Commanding the two girls to stay with him. He wanted them there when he woke up.

He calmed his heart which was pounding in his chest. Eventually, he was able to close his eyes and fall asleep.

Aza heard someone call his name.

Groggily, he yelled, "Go away."

Another knock, only louder.

The head of the Royal Guard was at the door.

"What do you want?" he said in an angry tone.

Then remembered he'd sent him to check on the prisoners.

"The prisoners are missing."

Aza jumped out of bed. Fully awake. "What do you mean 'missing'?"

"I went to the jail to check on the prisoners. As you commanded me to. Elias wasn't there. Neither was the Earthling. The cell was empty."

Aza wrung his hands and shook his head violently from side to side. He grabbed his head which was suddenly throbbing. "How is that possible?"

"I don't know."

"Where's the jailer who was watching them?" Aza screamed accusingly at the guard.

"He's gone too," the guard said hesitantly.

Aza screamed at the top of his lungs. The girls were awake as well and quickly grabbed their clothes and scurried out of the room before Aza could stop them.

Rage was building inside of him. His fists were clenched, an angry scowl formed, profanities were spewing out of his mouth mixed with spit.

I can't believe this is happening.

"How did they get away?"

"From the shaking, I guess," the guard said. "It damaged the foundation of the prison, and the cell doors all came off their hinges. They were wide open when I got there. All the prisoners escaped."

Aza grabbed a vase and threw it at the guard, nearly striking him in the head. He ducked just in time as the vase smashed against the wall shattering into many pieces.

"It's not my fault. The guard abandoned his post."

"He works for you! Have him killed," Aza shouted.

"I already sent someone to his house. He and his family have fled."

No!

"The jailer let them go free. I'll make him pay."

"I will find him."

"Track him down like a dog. Get men together. I want you to find Elias and Adam. Find them right now. Get them or you will answer to me with your life."

The guard hesitated.

"Now! Go. Don't come back without them."

Aza picked up another vase and started to throw it, but the guard was already gone.

9

Adam and Elias rushed to meet Jesus at Mount Shalam. Only stopping long enough for Elias to get cleaned up and assure his wife and family that he was safe.

She wanted him to change his shirt which was tattered and blood stained. Elias wanted to wear it. He felt it a badge of honor to have suffered for Christ.

After they left Elias' house, they kept one eye out for Aza and his men.

Elias was confident Jesus was still there. Adam had his doubts.

He still needed to work on his faith. Although the events at the prison had filled him with overwhelming joy. He had a pep to his step which he needed. Elias was older but Adam had to work to keep up with him.

Elias showed no ill effects from the last twenty-four hours.

Conversation was limited. They focused on practically running to Mount Shalam. Adam's mind was filled with distracting thoughts. When he left Earth more than three hundred years ago, how could he possibly have known what would transpire on the other side of the universe?

These had been the best of times in some ways, and the worst in others.

He had so many regrets. Here and on Earth. If only he could go back and start the journey over again. He'd do so many things differently. What he wouldn't give for one more conversation with Courtney. To tell her what he knew now.

To tell her he loved her.

Still after three hundred years.

He felt foolish.

Adam refused to let the thoughts dampen his mood. Going to meet Jesus was the most exciting thing that had ever happened to him. Even more than meeting God since he wasn't able to look upon God in the garden.

Jesus was present in the flesh. If he was still there. Adam would be so disappointed if they missed him.

Adam tried to remember everything he had read in the Bible. He wondered if the same scenarios would play out. The Bible said that God was the same yesterday, today, and forever. That made sense that God would interact with human beings in the same way on each planet.

Man acted similarly as well since they were created in the image of God, with the same evil thoughts, once sin entered the world. Jesus certainly seemed like the same man he'd read about in the Bible. The same compassion. If he really was Jesus, Adam intended to follow him to the end.

If?

Adam was kicking himself for having such little faith. He did everything he could do to tamp down the negative thoughts and feelings. When they neared Mount Shalam, they could see a group of men gathered but didn't see Jesus.

Adam didn't recognize any of them. Elias didn't know them either.

The greeting was joyous, nevertheless. For whatever reason, the men knew who they were.

"Welcome, Adam and Elias," one of them said.

"We heard you were in prison," another one chimed in.

They took turns hugging them. They couldn't help but notice Elias' shirt.

He shared with them how Adam came to rescue him. How God delivered them right at noon.

"Jesus said you'd be coming. That we were to wait for you."

"Where is Jesus?" Adam asked, nervously. "Did he leave?"

As if on cue, Jesus walked up and greeted them with a huge smile on his face. Which turned to a satisfied grin. Like he already knew what had happened to them. As if he had orchestrated their rescue. Maybe he did.

Jesus took Adam in his arms and pulled him close. Hugged him affectionately. It warmed Adam's heart.

He turned to the other men and said, "Adam and Elias, I want to introduce you to my other ten disciples."

"Other?" Adam said. "You mean..." He looked at Elias then at Jesus.

"That's right. I have chosen you and Elias to be my disciples as well as these ten men. You're the twelve I have chosen," Jesus said.

I can't believe Jesus chose me to be a disciple.

Over the next few days, Adam got to know the disciples very well. Lucas was his favorite. A physician by trade, he and Adam had the most in common. They spent hours discussing medicine and science. Lucas didn't have the formal training Adam had from universities, but Lucas was smart and instinctively seemed to know how to treat various ailments with success.

He examined Elias and gave him a clean bill of health. Couldn't even tell that he'd been beaten. Other than the blood on the shirt.

Jesus had Elias change the crimson-stained shirt. He had said, "Though your sins be as scarlet, I have made them white as snow."[1]

He added, "Because you are healed of the wounds and have a new body, you should wear a new shirt."

Martin and Tobi were brothers and farmers. Jed was a tax collector for King Joab's government. He'd walked away from his lucrative position when he met Jesus.

Liam was tall, strong, and muscular. As a soldier in Aza's inner circle, he had fought in many battles and had risen through the ranks. If there wasn't a price out on his head, there would be soon since he abandoned his post to follow Jesus.

The joker of the group was Abe, who liked to kid around. Adam told Abe some of his astronaut jokes, but Abe didn't get them. He had no reference point to understand why they were funny. He knew they were corny but didn't know why.

One day he came to Adam and said, "How do you get a baby astronaut to sleep?"

"How?"

"You rock-et." Abe roared, laughing. He'd made it up himself.

Adam enjoyed the banter. It reminded him of home.

Home. I still miss it, all these years later.

What I wouldn't give to see Courtney and Jamie again.

Three hundred years was a long time. Earth no longer existed. Still, a hollow longing in the pit of his stomach reminded him, he would never get over it. Someone laughing brought him back to reality.

Zach...

Zach was the good looking one. Jael, the wild one. Christopher, the quiet one. Everyone thought Ethan was Jesus' favorite. Including Ethan, who mentioned it several times. Jesus rebuked that idea when it came up, "I don't have any favorites. Whoever is first will be last anyway in the kingdom of heaven."[2]

The twelve became fast friends.

"No greater love has a man than to lay down his life for his friends," Jesus said.[3]

Adam knew what he meant. The other eleven didn't. They had no idea what was in store for them. What they'd be asked to sacrifice.

The road ahead wouldn't be easy, but Adam was up for the task. He would follow Jesus wherever the road took him—even to the point of death.

Which was exactly where they were headed. Adam didn't say anything to anyone. He'd been admonished by Jesus not to.

If their journey was anything like the twelve disciples on Earth, it'd be filled with miracles and times of great joy. And devastating hardships.

What an honor to be included with these men.

* * *

Jesus and the twelve disciples set out to the far territory away from Aza and his soldiers. Ethan's mother-in-law was sick with a fever, so they went to her house first, which was on the way. When they arrived at the house, the sickness was so severe, she'd become bedridden.

The moment Jesus touched her hand, healing flowed to her body. Immediately, she got up and made dinner for everyone.

Word spread. That evening, the people in the community brought many who were sick. By Jesus merely speaking a word over them, everyone who was sick received their healing.

Massive crowds began following them. The crowds were so big, Jesus had to stand on a hillside to teach to the multitudes. She lived by water and sometimes, he'd stand in a boat and preach from the sea.

He wouldn't leave until everyone was healed.

Jesus traveled through all the towns and villages of that area, teaching, and announcing the good news about the Kingdom. And he healed every kind of disease and illness. When he saw the crowds, he had compassion on them because they were confused and helpless, like sheep without a shepherd.

One night, the disciples were all sitting around a fire.

Jesus said, "I want to go to Gomor."

King Joab and Queen Zelbe, years before, had ordered that anyone with any kind of serious sickness, had to be removed to a city called Gomor. If someone had a skin condition, they were forced to live there. If anyone had a physical deformity, they were arrested and taken to Gomor. Anyone who was blind, deaf, or mute was rounded up and quarantined there.

Babies born with disabilities were taken from their parents and left there alone to die or to be cared for by the other infirmed. Armed guards surrounded the city to keep the people in. Their conditions were deplorable.

The king didn't provide them with any food or water. The people relied on friends and relatives bringing them what food they could spare.

Many people died every single day. A "U" was tattooed on their bodies, which stood for *unclean*. If they were sick, and came near another person, they had to yell, "Unclean! Unclean!" If they didn't, they were to be stoned to death. If they touched someone who wasn't unclean, then that person became unclean as well and had to go to the city, even if they weren't sick. No one could live there for very long before they became sick.

Everyone who could avoided that area. The moans and groans coming from the city could be heard for miles.

Liam, the former soldier, said, "I don't think it's a good idea. The city is guarded by King Joab's soldiers. Aza has put a price out for Adam and Elias's heads. Probably mine as well. Maybe all of us."

"I'm not afraid," Adam said. His faith had grown immeasurably from his time with Jesus.

"Neither am I," Elias said in agreement.

"The city is full of a lot of contagious diseases," Lucas, the physician, said. "If we go into the city, the guards won't let us out. We'll be considered unclean and won't be able to travel anywhere."

Jesus said, "The healthy don't need a physician. It's the sick who need a doctor."[4]

The next day, they set out for Gomor. The multitude followed them until they neared the city, and the crowd stopped before they got too close. They were afraid of the guards, and many of them had escaped out of the city and didn't want to be thrown back in. The others didn't want to be labeled unclean and forced into the city.

As they neared the city, Martin said to Tobi, his brother, "He's really going to do this. We're really going into the city. I hope he knows what he's doing."

The guards saw Jesus and a throng of people coming from a distance. They stood side by side to block the entrance.

Jesus walked right up to them.

"Arrest this man," one of the guards said, pointing at Jesus. "The king has a ransom out for him."

The guards moved toward Jesus and surrounded him.

Liam took out a knife and swung it at one of the guards slicing off his right ear.

10

The guard screamed in pain. Liam had chopped off his ear. The other guards drew their swords and prepared to fight.

Liam didn't back down.

He wasn't supposed to have a weapon. It was hidden in his belt.

"Enough of this," I said. While holding Liam back.

I walked over to the guard who was on his knee holding his head where his ear once was. I bent down on his knee next to him.

A guard came up from behind me and raised his sword in the air. Preparing to thrust it into my back.

Adam let out a scream. As did several of the other disciples.

"Don't you know that I could ask my Father for help and he'd send twelve armies of angels to protect me, and he would send them instantly?"[1] I said.

The guard didn't strike. He couldn't. His sword was raised in the air, but he couldn't move it. Couldn't force it down.

Angels were holding him back.

I ignored him. I reached on the ground and picked up the man's bloody ear. Placed it on his head and it was miraculously reattached. As if nothing had ever happened.

They were all amazed.

The disciples were murmuring among themselves.

"How did he do it?"

"Who is this man?"

I said to them, "Unless you see signs and wonders will you not believe?"[2]

The guards became afraid and took off running. Even the one who was healed. Leaving the gate to the city unguarded.

"They saw signs and wonders and yet did not believe in me or in the one who sent me."

We entered through the gate.

My heart broke with the human suffering I saw at Gomor. I grieved that men could treat other men, women, and children so inhumanely. While I wanted everyone to be saved and come to know me as their Savior, I gravitated toward the oppressed, the hurting, sick, weak, and dying.

Their souls were without hope. I wanted to bring them hope.

My intention was for every single person in the entire city to be completely healed. I would not leave until that was accomplished.

I started out walking through the city and motioned for my disciples to follow me. They did so cautiously. They didn't yet realize I would protect them, but I understood. I had to help their unbelief. They'd seen me heal many who were sick, and yet they were afraid of getting sick as if I couldn't heal them.

I spent most of my time with them for that reason. I wouldn't be with them much longer. When I am gone, they must do the same works that I do, only more. Today would be a day for building their faith. Many miracles were going to take place right in front of their eyes.

The multitudes weren't sure why I was there and cowered away at first. I felt so bad for them.

"Do you want to be well?" I would say to each group of people I met.

As each group was healed, they swarmed around me like children about to be given candy.

The power of the Holy Spirit was strong in me. I could feel his healing touch flow through me to each person as they were healed from their infirmities. Seeing the looks on their faces brought me great joy as the healing power of my Father flowed through me into their bodies.

The look on their faces. The smiles.

A throng of people gathered and pressed in against me. Suddenly, a woman came up and touched my garment, and I felt the power flow out of me and into her body.

I turned to the crowd and said, "Who touched me?"[3]

One of the disciples answered, "What do you mean, who touched you? Look at this huge crowd. Many people are touching you."

My eyes swept over the crowd, looking for the lady I knew had touched me. She would be afraid, and I wanted to reassure her.

The woman who experienced the miracle came up to me, trembling with fear. She threw herself down at my feet and said with a shaky voice, "I'm the one who touched you."

Her head was down. She was afraid to look at me.

"I heard a voice inside saying if I just touched your garment I would be healed," she said, barely above a whisper.

She hesitated, but I looked at her with encouragement to continue.

"I pressed in, but I couldn't get close enough to touch you. I was desperate. I have suffered from this for twelve years."

She began to cry.

"I pushed through the crowd. I'm sorry. I cut in front of some of you." She reached and touched several people around her.

She began to speak more confidently. "I reached for your garment, but you moved away too fast. I kept pressing in. I thought I wasn't going to be able to make it."

She paused. "Then suddenly, you slowed down. I still couldn't reach you, so I got on my hands and knees and crawled until I could touch the hem at the bottom of your garment. When I touched it, the sickness was gone."

She was sobbing now.

I reached down, took her hand, and lifted her up. I wiped away her tears with a piece of my garment.

I said to her, "Daughter, because you dared to believe, your faith has healed you. Go with peace in your heart and be free from your suffering."

She screamed with joy.

It made me so happy.

We went from place to place and I healed the sick. I walked through the entire city again making sure we hadn't missed anyone.

As we were beginning to leave, I looked over and saw Adam on his knee talking to a woman who was crying. I walked over to find out what was happening.

* * *

Adam noticed a young girl, barely fifteen years old, if that, sitting alone, crying. Her golden blonde hair was matted and caked with dirt. She looked as if she hadn't eaten in days. He walked over and knelt on one knee beside her. Everyone else around them were laughing and rejoicing, having been healed by Jesus. This young girl was the only one not participating in the celebration. Adam wanted to find out why.

He took her hand.

She pulled it away.

"What's wrong?" he asked.

She didn't answer.

"How come you didn't go to Jesus and be healed." She didn't appear to have any obvious physical ailment, but he asked the question anyway.

"I'm not sick. At least not physically." She said the last part sarcastically.

Jesus walked up but motioned for Adam to continue what he was saying.

"Why are you crying?" Adam asked.

"I'm ashamed."

"Of what? Why are you ashamed?"

She looked at Jesus and then at Adam. She appeared unsure whether to say anything, like she didn't trust them. Finally, the words came.

"Some soldiers came to my house and dragged me away. My momma was screaming at them. She tried to stop them, but they hurt her. My dad and brothers are gone, made to work for the king."

Adam reached up with his sleeve and wiped the tears off the side of her face, leaving a stain on his shirt from where the tears had mixed with the grime.

She continued. "They took me to the palace. I became one of the king's slaves. King Joab."

She said his name with disdain in her voice.

"Other girls were there ... They dressed us in clothes that barely covered us. One night, the king's son, Aza ... "

Adam stiffened. Just the mention of Aza's name sent fury through Adam like a raging fire.

I should have known he was behind this.

Jesus put his hand on Adam's shoulder as if he knew what he was thinking.

The girl continued. "Aza took me to his room. The king gave me to him as a present. Like I was his possession ... Eww. I guess I am ... was."

A far-away look came over her.

"He made me do the most disgusting things. I was a virgin. Not anymore. The next morning, he tried to make me do the same things again. I refused."

She bit her lower lip.

"I told him no. He fought me, but I fought him off. He fell and hurt his arm. That made him so mad. I ran away. The soldiers caught me. They beat me. Aza sent me here. Said I would die here."

Tears welled up in her eyes again.

"I can't go back home. I'm so ashamed of what I've done."

Adam looked up at Jesus, wanting him to say something to the girl. Instead, all he said was, "You're doing fine, Adam."

"I know all about feeling ashamed," Adam said softly. "If anyone should feel ashamed, it's me. You didn't do anything to be ashamed of. Those men should be ashamed, not you."

He reached over and lifted her chin so she would look at him. "In Christ, there is no shame."

"But I feel so guilty."

"There's no condemnation to those in Christ."[4]

The Bible verses flooded back into Adam's mind like a river.

"No man would ever want me now. I'm unclean."

She showed Adam the "U" tattooed on her arm.

"If you are in Christ, you are a new creation, and the old things are passed away, all things become new."[5]

"Really?" Her countenance brightened.

"Yes." Adam said, finally believing it himself. "Your past is behind you. Nothing you have done can separate you from the love of God."

She threw her arms around Adam. "I want so much for that to be true." She didn't let go.

Lucas walked up and said to Jesus, "The people are starving. We need to give them food."

"Go ahead and feed them," Jesus said.

"We don't have any money. There's no way to feed everybody. I don't want to send them on their way, though. They might faint on the way home. Many are still weak. Some have been in Gomor for years."

"Adam, after we eat, you and Elias take this girl back to her family."

Jesus turned back to Lucas. "Lucas, tell all the people to sit down over there, on the hill." He pointed. "I will be right there."

Jesus turned back to the girl. He lifted the back of her shirt. On her back were stripes where she'd been beaten. Jesus touched her back and the stripes disappeared. He touched her arm and the "U" branded on her arm disappeared, as did the brand on every person in the entire city.

A roar went up from the crowd as they realized what had happened.

Jesus lifted the girl to her feet and said, "Whoever believes in me will never be put to shame. Do you believe in me?"[6]

The girl nodded her head yes.

"Are you hungry?" Jesus asked.

"I'm famished."

"Go sit down on the hill."

She ran off with a new spring to her step. Like a whole new person.

Which was what she was.

Maybe Adam was too.

11

This was always one of my favorite miracles.

The crowd was sitting on the side of a mountain. My disciples watched in anticipation. Not having any idea what was about to happen.

All but Adam, of course. He had a silly grin on his face. He knew how I fed the five thousand on Earth with five loaves and two fish and figured I was about to do the same thing on Adon.

I always did this miracle on all the planets. As much as anything else, it brought glory to my father which was always my first purpose.

The crowd from Gomer had also grown faint. From months and years of starvation and from listening to me teach for hours in the hot sun. They needed food and water.

I was almost done teaching.

"Don't worry about your life, what you eat, or about your body."[1]

I paused to let that sink in. The crowd was so large, I had to speak loudly for them to hear me.

"Life is more than food. Consider the birds in the air."

I pointed to the sky. A number of birds flew over the throng of people. Anticipating scraps of leftover food.

"The birds don't have storehouses. They don't have barns. They don't sow food in the ground or harvest it. Yet they still eat. How? God feeds them."

The crowd cheered.

"How much more valuable are you than birds?"

Another cheer erupted.

I could tell they were hungry, but still enthusiastic.

"Are you hungry?"

"Yes!" The loudest cheer of all.

"My God shall supply all your needs, according to his riches in glory."[2]

The crowd was standing and cheering. I raised my hand to silence them.

"Go ahead and be seated. I'm going to feed you now."

The disciples didn't say anything, but I knew what they were thinking. How was I going to feed all those people with such little food?

It was time.

"Adam, give me the seven packets of food."[3]

He and the other disciples were standing near me. To my right.

He took them out of a satchel and handed them to me. I took them in my hands, looked up to heaven, and thanked God for the food, blessing it. As was my custom. I always thanked God for his provision of food before I ate it. My followers should always do the same.

I turned to the disciples.

"Each of you take a basket and distribute the food to the people," I said.

"What baskets?" Abe asked.

"The ones right behind you."

They turned to look and let out a gasp.

"Where did those come from?" Martin the farmer asked.

"From my Father in heaven."

When they each picked up a basket, it was full of loaves and fishes. Much to their amazement.

Each time they came back with an empty basket, they found full baskets next to me. All the people ate until they were satisfied. Hundreds of baskets of food were left over and were distributed to the people to take with them.

"Are you thirsty?" I asked the crowd.

"Yes!"

"Bring me pitchers of water," I said to the disciples.

"Where will we find them?" Lucas the physician asked.

"Behind you," I said.

I blessed the water and told them to let each person drink from the pitcher until everyone was no longer thirsty.

"The pitcher will run dry after two or three people," Christopher said. Even though he was the quiet one, he was standing next to Jesus and asked what the others were thinking.

I let out a sigh. I had to be patient with them.

"Did you not just see what Jesus did with the food?" Adam asked. "He'll do the same with the water."

I smiled. Happy to see Adam's faith growing.

When everyone had enough to drink, I then began to preach again. I held a loaf of bread in the air.

"I am the bread of life; he who comes to me will not hunger."[4]

I raised a glass of water in the air.

"Whoever drank from the pitchers of water, will be thirsty again. In a few minutes or hours. Whoever drinks the water I give him will never thirst. That water springs up from a fountain into everlasting life."[5]

The disciples were murmuring among themselves.

"Does that mean that they will never have to eat or drink again?" Lucas asked.

"No. It means Jesus is going to give them all a basket and pitcher and it will never run dry," Abe said.

"It's a spiritual metaphor," Adam said. "It means that food and water only satisfy for a short period of time. In Jesus is the spiritual food and water that will last us for an eternity."

"You said it well, Adam."

He beamed from my encouragement.

I preached for several more hours. The crowd was sent home with my blessing to reunite with their loved ones in Adon.

When we were alone, I went up the hillside to pray. The disciples followed me. When I sat down at the top, I gave them instructions.

"Here are the towns I plan to visit. I am sending two of you to each town to prepare the way for my arrival."[6]

"What are we to do if we run into soldiers?" Liam asked.

"Some of you will run into them."

"What are we to do?" Liam asked. "You told us not to carry a weapon."

"Don't stop to greet anyone on the road," I said. "When you find a town that is peaceful, stay there."

"What are we to eat and drink?" Lucas asked. "Are you sending us with a basket full of food and a pitcher of water?"

I shook my head. "When you find a city that's peaceful, find a home where the people will feed you and provide you with shelter. Don't move from house to house. Stay in one place. Eat and drink whatever they put in front of you. Always bless it first. Accept their hospitality. Bless their home and town."

"What if we can't find anyone who is peaceful?" Liam asked.

"If the town refuses to welcome you, wipe the dust off your feet and abandon them to their fate."

"What is their fate?" Adam asked.

"Do you remember Sodom and Gomorrah?" I asked him.

He nodded.

"I tell you, it will be more bearable on that day for Sodom than for that town."[7]

"What is Sodom, Adam?" Jeb the tax gatherer asked. He still couldn't believe that Jesus and the disciples trusted him with the treasury.

Adam answered correctly. "It's an ancient city on earth. Known for its depravity. They were worse than Queen Zelbe and King Joab, if you can believe that."

"What happened to the city?" Ethan asked.

"God destroyed it with fire from heaven. Nothing was left of it," Adam answered.

"Wow!"

"Is that going to happen on Adon?" Liam asked.

I changed the subject.

"Don't concern yourself with that for now," I said. "You need to focus on preaching the good news. Tell them what you have seen. The blind can see. Ears can hear. The lame can walk. Every person in Gomer was healed."

"What if they don't believe us? You won't be there to perform miracles," Lucas asked. Being a physician, he had a hard time wrapping his mind around the miracles. At first, he tried to come up with a logical explanation. At some point, he gave up. When he looked foolish trying to explain them away.

"You can do everything you saw me do," I said. "You have that power within you. You will do even greater things than I do."[8]

"How is that possible?" Lucas asked.

"With God, all things are possible to those who believe. Does the woman in Gomer who touched my garment have more faith than you?"

"No!"

"Even the demons will submit to my name."

The disciples knew what demons were. We'd encountered many of them in Gomer and along the journey. I pointed them out to them whenever we confronted them.

I continued. "Do good to those who hate you. Respect and give thanks for those who try to bring bad to you. Pray for those who make it hard for you."[9]

Liam interrupted. "Jesus, you saw the crowds. They are with you. We could gather an army of thousands and march on the city and overthrow the king and queen. We can set up a reign. You can be the king."

He had so much to learn.

"That's not why I have come to Adon."

"I don't understand. Wouldn't it be a good thing to end the reign of the evil king and queen. They are killing the prophets. Oppressing the people. I once was one of them. I know what they do to innocent and helpless people. I did my share of beating and killing."

Liam's voice trailed off in shame as he said it.

"Whoever hits you on one side of the face, turn so he can hit you on the other."[10]

"That's not happening," Liam said. His back was bowed and his head up in defiance. "If someone hits me, I'm hitting him back."

"If he takes your coat, give him your shirt also."

"I'd like to see him take my coat."

"Do you love me, Liam?"

"You know I do, Jesus. Do you love me?"

"Yes."

"We all love you," the other disciples said.

"If you love someone who loves you, what's so special about that?" I asked. "Even King Joab and Queen Zelbe love those people who love them."

"They aren't capable of real love," Liam argued. "They don't love the soldiers. They use them. To stay in power."

"That's my point. They love those who serve them. As Christians, we love because God first loved us. Here's what makes you different from them."

"What?"

"Love those who hate you."

"I don't know if I can."

I didn't rebuke him. They'd only been with me a short time. The things of God were hard to understand. I wasn't coming to set up a kingdom on Adon, but an eternal kingdom, in heaven.

"God is love. If you don't love then you don't know God."[11]

"We want to know God."

"To know me is to know God. This is love. Not that we love God, but that he loved us and sent his son to atone for your sins."

The disciples had so many more questions. I was weary, but I answered them all. After many more hours, they rested, preparing to leave on their journeys the next morning.

I knew sorrow would await many of them.

12

Jesus instructed Elias and Jeb, the tax collector, to go to Center City. Home for both of them, but the seat of power for Queen Zelbe and King Joab. The most dangerous of all the towns assigned.

Elias was excited.

Adam was furious but didn't dare question Jesus to his face.

A heated debate broke out among the disciples after Jesus left them. He was somewhere on the mountain praying. Out of earshot.

"That's suicide," Adam argued. "You'll both be killed."

"I'm not afraid," Elias answered.

Jeb didn't seem as confident. His was a difficult situation. The common people hated him. He had been ruthless in collecting the taxes. Always charging more than required and pocketing it for himself. While he'd given away all of his massive fortune to the poor when he decided to follow Jesus, some people would tear him apart limb by limb if given the opportunity.

The authorities wanted him dead as well. Since he had abandoned his post, a bounty was out on his head. Joab ordered him arrested the moment he stepped foot back in the city.

Adam was right. Going back to Center City was like sending them to their deaths.

That didn't faze Elias. He was almost giddy. Excited to see his family but even more excited to preach in the city square. Where they had captured him the first time.

"I can't wait to see the look on Joab's face when I'm brought before him. He'll think he's seen a ghost. Zelbe's teeth will fall out of her head."

Everyone laughed. Everyone except Adam. He was beside himself.

"This isn't funny, Elias. They'll kill you. You know that."

"They can't kill me unless God allows it."

"Elias is right. We have to trust Jesus," Lucas, the physician said.

"I should be the one who goes to Center City," Liam, the soldier said. He had been lamenting the fact that Jesus was sending him to a peaceful region. Where there'd be no threats at all. Where his temper wouldn't get him in trouble. Probably the reason why Jesus was sending him there.

"It's not safe for you either. The king and queen want you dead as well," Adam said.

"At least I know how to defend myself," he retorted.

"We don't have to defend ourselves," Elias said. "Remember what Jesus said. We are not to worry about what we say. When the time comes, we'll be given the words. The Spirit of the Father will be speaking through us."

"What good will words do against swords and knives?" Liam argued.

The disciples seemed split. They were arguing among themselves.

"Liam's right," Adam said. "You were already arrested and beaten once, Elias. I won't be there to rescue you a second time."

"You rescued me?" Elias said, with a chuckle. "The Spirit of God was the one who freed us from our chains. Right at noon. It couldn't have been a coincidence."

Anger rose up in Adam. He had risked his life going into that dungeon and it sounded like Elias didn't appreciate it.

"You're forgetting it was *my* idea to believe God to free us at noon."

Adam felt foolish as soon as he said it. If not for God, they'd both probably already be dead.

"Don't be ridiculous," Abe said, voicing how Adam felt. "Adam, you didn't have anything to do with it. God was the one who caused the quake."

Abe was right, but the comment still stung and made Adam angry.

"I didn't see you there!" Adam said. "Risking your life."

"I didn't even know Elias back then," Abe said. "I would've been there if I'd known."

Normally the jokester in the bunch, it took a lot to get Abe angry.

Abe was standing in a fighting stance. Adam took one step toward him. Lucas got between them. Not that they would've come to blows, but the tension was so thick, they might've said something they regretted.

Adam wished he hadn't brought it up. He looked around for Jesus. The last thing he wanted was for him to hear them and come over and admonish him.

The whole argument was his fault.

"Calm down. All of you," Christopher, the usually quiet one said. "What good does it do to fight among ourselves?"

"Do you want them both to die, Christopher?" Martin, the farmer said. Taking a pause from his own argument with his brother, Tobi, to let his feelings be known.

"Of course not," Christopher answered. "But Jesus said we'd face persecution. That we'd be handed over to local councils. We're all going to get flogged, eventually."

Adam shuddered. He remembered the wounds on Elias's back. He'd already figured his day was coming. When he'd have to suffer for Christ.

At least he deserved it. Since he was the one who ate the apple.

Before the shame could overwhelm Adam, Ethan said, "Remember what Jesus said, everyone. Don't fear the one who can kill your body but can't touch your soul. Fear the one who is able to destroy both soul and body in hell."[1]

Adam was already afraid of that. He knew full well that's what he deserved.

"I'm prepared to suffer for Jesus," Jeb said. Mustering up some courage. "That's what we all signed up for."

Jeb had a past too, but at least he admitted he was a thief. Adam had never admitted to eating the apple. Adam admired his bravery.

Adam looked around the campfire. The anger fell off him. These were good men. He'd give his life for any of them. They were already like brothers. Since Adam never had any siblings on Earth, he felt a real bond with them.

He wished Jesus would send him to Center City. Alone. If not alone, at least let him go with Elias.

Part of him wanted to go find Jesus and try to talk him out of sending Elias to Center City. Adam was afraid of that too. Not sure what Jesus' reaction would be. He'd probably say he lacked faith.

Everyone sat back down, and the tone turned more somber.

"Christopher is right. We'll all be flogged and probably killed someday," Zach said.

"I'm ready," Elias said.

"They may not kill you, but they can arrest you," Adam said. "They'll take you before the High Council."

"I hope they do. I'll preach to them."

"They won't let you."

"I'd like to see them try and stop me."

"That's what I'm afraid of," Adam said, his voice cracking as he said it. He knew his friend. He'd march right into the city square at the first opportunity and start shouting the gospel at the top of his lungs. Until he attracted everyone's attention.

Including the soldiers.

Elias stood and walked over and sat beside Adam. He put his arm on Adam's shoulder. "Don't be afraid."

"I'm not afraid for myself," Adam said. "I'm afraid for you. It doesn't seem worth the risk. Zach is right. You should go to a city that will welcome you. Where thousands would be saved. You're a great preacher. How will it help the kingdom if you're dead?"

"God's ways may seem foolish to men," Elias said. "Jesus told me to go and that's what I'm going to do. It's decided."

Adam started to object.

"Is the student above the teacher?" Elias stated firmly.

Adam remained quiet. Clearly thinking it best to quit arguing. Elias was right. Who was he to question Jesus?

By that time, they were all exhausted and decided to go to sleep. The next morning, they ate a final meal together, and prepared to go their separate ways.

When the time came, Adam embraced Elias and held it. He loved him.

Tears flowed down his cheeks.

"Don't worry my friend," Elias said. "God's will be done on Adon as it is in heaven."

"I'll be praying for you."

"Thank you. I'll be praying for you as well. For all of you," Elias said with a wave of his hand to the rest of the disciples.

Adam looked around.

Where was Jesus?

He hadn't even come to say goodbye.

Adam watched his friend head west. Until they were out of sight.

Adam was going west as well, but not as far as Center City. Farther south. On a different road.

I have a bad feeling about this.

He wondered if he'd ever see his friend again.

* * *

Three days later

Word got back to the king that the entire city of Gomor had been emptied by Jesus and his disciples. The guards fled their posts and Jesus freed all the people. The king was furious. He considered it treason.

King Joab called in his High Council to discuss the problem. Joab wanted Jesus and all the disciples killed.

Queen Zelbe blamed the king for letting Elias and Adam escape from prison. Joab blamed Zelbe for always being off somewhere with her lover. Aza didn't want to open his mouth for fear they'd blame him.

He was actually the one who had let Adam and Elias escape from prison. Even though it wasn't his fault, his parents didn't see it that way.

"This Jesus is turning the people against us," the king said. "Jesus must die."

Most of the members clapped in approval.

Aza was nervous. He'd heard about the crowds around Jesus. If he tried to arrest him, the throng would overwhelm his soldiers.

One member of the High Council stood and said, "Men, take care what you are planning to do to these men. This will die out on its own. People are following Jesus now, and if we kill him, we will make him a martyr, and the people may rise up against us. So, my advice is to leave them alone. If this is not from God, it will die out soon, and the people will tire of this false prophet. If it's of God, you will not be able to stop it. You may even find yourselves fighting against God."[2]

"We can't just let them speak freely against us," Queen Zelbe insisted. "I agree with the king. They all must die."

Aza spoke up. "There's nothing we can do about it. They're all over in the eastern district right now. Thousands of people are following them. We can't get close enough to arrest them. We need someone, anyone close to Jesus, who will betray him and tell us when he is alone."

About that moment, a soldier in Aza's army came running into the room. "Elias is preaching in the city square right now," he said excitedly.

"Is Jesus with him?" Joab asked.

"No. It's only him and one other."

"What's the size of the crowd?"

"A few dozen. They just arrived there. I came right away."

Aza's heart did somersaults. He had more than enough soldiers.

"Go and seize him," Zelbe said to her son.

Aza left immediately.

Several of his soldiers followed him.

A few minutes later, he returned with Elias bound in ropes.

13

Elias stood before the High Council and Joab declared that he was on trial for treason. A number of witnesses came forward to speak against Elias.

"Elias said Jesus will destroy this place. He has come to take over the kingdom and make himself the king."

Another said, "Elias was speaking against the Queen."

Elias stood there defiantly with his hands and feet bound by ropes. Waiting for the Holy Spirit to give him the words to say.

One of the council men spoke up, "His face looks like the face of an angel. Are you sure he is saying these things?"[1]

The council was torn. The king was trying to build a consensus to kill Elias before he ordered it. For more than twenty minutes, a parade of witnesses came before them. Mostly spewing venomous lies. No doubt paid to do so.

"Elias, what do you have to say for yourself?" the king asked. Up until then, Elias had remained silent, not answering the false accusations.

The Spirit of the Lord suddenly came rushing on him.

"God has this complaint against you," Elias said. "You tolerate this woman—Zelbe. She teaches the people to commit sexual sin. God has given her time to repent, and she refuses."

Zelbe lunged at Elias, but Joab held her back.

"What more do you need to hear?" Zelbe cried out in a loud voice.

The king turned to the council members. "Didn't I tell you that he never prophesies anything good about us, only bad?"

"God is going to throw Zelbe on a bed of suffering," Elias continued. "Those who commit adultery with her will suffer greatly. She is an abomination to the Lord. Because you tolerate her, Joab, you will die as well."[2]

When Queen Zelbe heard that, she was so furious with Elias that her face distorted with rage.

The king had heard enough as well.

Zelbe implored Aza, "Kill Elias. Strike the fear of Zelbe on all of them. Jesus too."

Most of the council shouted in agreement with Zelbe.

"You stubborn people!" Elias spoke up boldly, throwing more fire on their burning rage. "You are heathens at heart and deaf to the truth. Must you resist God forever?"

The tension in the room was at a fever pitch.

"God has put a deceiving spirit in him."

"He has gone mad."

"Kill him!"

Elias was defiant and unafraid. He had to shout to be heard over the din.

"You were all alive when God was among us in the Garden of Eden. God provided us food from heaven, and there was no sin. We all saw God's goodness for centuries. Everyone was happy and could walk these streets with no fear."

"Who ate the fruit?" Zelbe yelled. "Do you know?"

The room turned silent.

Elias answered calmly.

"Someone ate the apple, and death entered Adon. But that person is not the only one to blame. We have all disobeyed God's laws and none of us is righteous. Our righteousness is but filthy rags before God. But God has sent the Son of Man, Jesus, to save us from our sins. Repent and believe in the Lord Jesus Christ, and you will be saved."

The members of the High Council placed their hands over their ears. They shook their fists at Elias in rage. They yelled, "Stone him! Stone him!"

Joab ordered it.

Aza seized Elias and dragged him into the city square near where Adam and Eve were killed. The soldiers gathered stones.

As they stoned him, Elias prayed, "Lord Jesus, receive my spirit. Forgive them. Don't charge them with this sin."[3]

And with that, he died.

Jeb stood at a distance. He had fled when the soldiers came to arrest them. When he saw that Elias was dead, he felt deep anguish. He went out from there and hanged himself.[4]

Elias was buried the same day in a grave given to them by a rich man. A member of the High Council, who had been present for Elias's trial and stoning. So moved by Elias's words and demeanor, he believed them and became a follower of Christ.

Benjamin sent his two sisters to tell Jesus of their father's death and to urge him to come. They returned and reported that Jesus told them he would come when he could. He had his Father's work to tend to.

They set the funeral for four days later to give Jesus time to come.

* * *

Four days later

Adam rushed to Center City when he learned of Elias' death. All the other disciples had returned as well, even though they were in grave danger.

The day of Elias's funeral came, and Jesus wasn't there.

A huge throng gathered to honor Elias.

Aza and some of his soldiers were standing at a distance. They hadn't approached Adam, probably because the people would have torn them to shreds.

Elias was buried in a cave. The people crowded around to honor the prophet of God and to hear the speakers.

Sophie asked Adam if he would say a few words.

Adam looked over the crowd and took in a deep breath. Fighting back tears.

"As you know, I'm not from here. I traveled a great distance to this planet. Elias was the first person I met on Adon. I wasn't in very good shape when I met him."

Adam's voice cracked. He tried to compose himself. The images of his burned face and the right side of his body popped into his head. He'd had a fire on the spacecraft and was burned badly. He almost didn't land on Adon. Once the fire happened and he was running out of oxygen, he had no choice.

It was probably fate. God wanted him to discover Adon.

Adam took a deep breath and continued. "God told Elias to come find me. Imagine my surprise when he showed up on the doorstep of my spacecraft. He must've thought I was an alien. I guess I was."

A chuckle went through the crowd.

"Elias wasn't afraid. He wasn't afraid then, and he wasn't afraid on the day he died. Elias wanted to come to Center City. He wanted to preach in the square and before the High Council. He wasn't afraid of the soldiers."

Adam said it loud enough for Aza to hear.

"Neither am I."

The crowd erupted in applause.

Adam was struggling with the words. He was supposed to be honoring his friend. Instead, he was stoking the rage of Aza and the soldiers. He didn't care. If he could, he'd go back to the spacecraft and retrieve a weapon and kill them all.

Where was Jesus?

He still wasn't there.

"I didn't think I could find the words to do my friend justice."

Adam wished the Spirit of the Lord would come upon him and give him the words to say. He was babbling on. Hardly making sense.

"All I can do is tell you how we met. How I knew him. How he touched my life. Forever. I will miss you, old friend."

His friend's death was too painful to express in words. He felt anger that Jesus sent Elias to Center City. Adam knew this would happen.

He felt even more angry that Jesus wasn't there. Maybe he was afraid of the soldiers. That didn't seem like the Jesus Adam had read about in the Bible.

Why else wouldn't he be there?

The grief and the anger were in a raging battle inside of Adam to see which one would have dominance. Right now, the anger was winning out.

Several other people related a few funny stories about Elias and shared some particularly poignant memories of Elias and his faithfulness to God.

Another man, who witnessed the stoning, stood up and shared how Elias was faithful to God even to the end, even asking God to forgive those who were stoning him.

A sudden movement.

At a distance. It startled Adam.

Aza and his soldiers had their swords raised.

Some of the crowd was running. Adam stood up on a rock to look to see what all the commotion was about.

Jesus.

He had arrived. The crowd was pressing around him. Aza and the soldiers kept their distance.

Jesus pressed through the crowd and walked to the front, near the tomb.

Their eyes met. Guilt was churning inside of Adam like an eddy. The look on Jesus' face wasn't condemning.

He walked up to Adam and embraced him. Adam felt the warmth inside.

Benjamin said to Jesus, "Lord, if you had been there, my father would not have died."[5]

Jesus said, "I'm glad I wasn't there, for now you will really believe me."

The crowd murmured amongst themselves. "Why did he say he was glad he wasn't there? That doesn't make sense."

Jesus must have sensed their confusion because he said, "You will see God's glory if you will believe."

He stood up on the rock where Adam had been standing so the entire crowd could hear him, and in a loud voice, he said, "I am the resurrection and the life. Anyone who believes in me will never die."

"Do you believe this, Sophie?" Jesus said. Sophie was Elias's wife. Her eyes were red from crying.

Sophie said, "I believe, Lord."

"Your husband will rise again."

"I know Lord. He'll rise when everyone else rises on the last day, like you taught us."

Jesus turned to Adam and said, "Go and roll the stone away from the grave."

A gasp went up from the crowd.

He instructed the other disciples to help him.

Sophie said, "My husband has been dead for four days. The smell will be terrible."

Jesus responded, "Didn't I tell you that you would see God's glory if you believe?"

Adam, Benjamin, and two of the disciples rolled the stone aside. The stone was so large it took four of them to move it.

Jesus looked up to heaven and said, "Father, thank you for hearing me. You always hear me, but I said it out loud for the sake of all these people standing here, so they will believe you sent me."

Then Jesus shouted, "Elias, come out!"

A hush came over the crowd. Everyone turned their gaze to the entrance of the tomb.

For several seconds, nothing happened. Finally, Elias came out of the tomb, staggering. His feet were bound by the graveclothes, and his face was covered.

"Unwrap him and set him free," Jesus told them.

The other disciples rushed to Elias and removed his graveclothes.

Great joy came upon everyone.

They ran to Elias and hugged and kissed him. Sophie embraced Elias and wouldn't let go of him until her daughters and sons insisted that they should have a turn. The whole family gathered in one big hug.

All the injuries from the stoning were completely healed, and Elias was back to his old self.

Adam grabbed Elias and held him in a huge bear hug. Everyone was laughing, singing, dancing, and glorifying God. They thanked Jesus profusely.

Jesus stayed with them for a little while and then left. A big party was held at Elias' house that night.

Aza stood at a distance. Adam could hear him swearing.

14

The next day, Elias was back preaching in the center square. Adam and the disciples were with him. Many miracles happened among the people. The sick came and were healed. If the shadow of one of the disciples fell on a person who was sick, they were immediately healed. The number who were followers of Jesus grew daily.

For the time being, the king and queen left them alone. Probably because they were afraid of the people.

One day, Joab sent for Elias. The disciples didn't want him to go alone, so they all went with him.

Joab had developed a cough. He was afraid it was something serious. He had commanded that no one touch Elias or the disciples because he wanted Elias to heal him of the infirmity.

Aza stood next to the king. Zelbe wasn't there. Elias stood before the king with the disciples standing off to the side.

The king asked, "Am I going to die?"

"Yes," Elias answered. "You have sold yourself to do evil in the sight of the Lord. Zelbe is going to die as well. Dogs are going to eat her body on the streets."[1]

Aza lifted his sword and lunged forward like he was going to attack Elias. But Joab held him back.

Joab began to cough violently from the exertion.

"Can you do anything to save me?" Joab asked, when he finally caught his breath.

Elias tried but was unable to heal him. Joab was angry because the cough persisted.

"Speak to Jesus, maybe he will heal me," the king implored Elias.

Elias said, "Speak to Jesus yourself. Maybe he will show mercy toward you. If you believe in him, you will have eternal life."

"I can live forever?" Joab said. "I can become like God?"

He apparently thought it meant he would never die and become like a God.

"I want to meet Jesus," Joab said. "Go and get him. He has my word that no harm will come to him or to any of his disciples."

The disciples left, found Jesus, and brought him back to stand before the king.

The king said, "Good teacher, Elias said that I could have eternal life. What do I need to do?"

"Why do you call me good?" Jesus asked. "No one is good except God alone. However, do not murder, do not commit adultery, do not steal, do not bear false witness, do not defraud others, and honor your father and mother."[2]

"I have done all of those things all of my life."

Adam rolled his eyes.

Before the fall, everyone was perfect. No one had sinned. For the last thirty years, Joab had pushed the limits of depravity.

Jesus looked Joab in the eyes and said to him, "One thing you are missing. Go and sell everything you have and give it all to the poor. You will then have treasures in heaven and in the life to come."

Joab was extremely saddened because he was a very rich man, so he sent Jesus away. Joab had accumulated a great deal of possessions on the backs of the people and was the wealthiest man on Adon.

When they were with Jesus privately, Elias asked Jesus, "Why was I not able to heal him?"

"You of little faith. This can only come about with prayer."[3]

He instructed them on the importance of prayer and fasting. On how to strengthen their faith.

A few weeks later, King Joab died.

Word got back to the disciples that on his deathbed, the king made Aza swear that he would avenge his death. His last words were, "Jesus healed a lot of people. He could have healed me, but he wouldn't. I want you to make sure he pays for that."

Two weeks later, Adam learned Zelbe had died. One of her lovers discovered her with another man the night before and threw her out the window of the palace, and her blood splattered on the ground. Dogs were seen eating her body off the streets exactly as Elias had predicted.

Aza became king.

He continued to do evil in the sight of the Lord and was even worse than his parents. He persecuted the followers of Jesus with even more ruthlessness. He didn't touch Adam, Jesus, or his disciples but was becoming more brazen in his opposition to them.

They remained in the center district, preaching the gospel. The district had the most people, and this seemed like the best opportunity to reach them.

Now there was a member of the High Council, a man named Nicholas, who was a teacher of the law. Aza had formed a new church on Adon and took some of the teachings of Jesus and incorporated them into a church based on a false teaching of grace.

Of course, he made himself the head of the church.

His father Joab taught that people had to obey the laws that he had established for them. That salvation came by following the king's commands given to him by God.

He didn't follow them himself. Neither did Aza who was even sleeping with one of his brothers' wives.

Jesus and his disciples taught that salvation came from grace through faith, not based on our works but on the works of Christ.

"For God so loved Adon," the disciples taught, "that he sent his only begotten son, Jesus. That whoever would believe in him wouldn't perish but have eternal life."[4]

The new Church of Adon was just the opposite. They taught that the people should go on sinning. So that they could receive more grace.

Jesus' followers were growing, but Aza's even more so. The people were loving the new-found freedom from the law. Being able to sin with no consequences.

Nicholas came to Jesus one night and said, "Jesus, we know that you have come from God. No one could perform these miracles if God was not with him."[5]

Adam didn't trust Nicholas. He wondered if he was only saying those things to trick Jesus into trusting him. He was certain Jesus wouldn't fall for it.

"How can I see the kingdom of God?" Nicholas asked.

Jesus replied, "You must be born again."

"How can I be born a second time? I can't go back to my mother's womb."

Nicholas was more than three thousand years old. Before the fall, no one died. They all lived in a world without sickness and disease. God protected them from accidents. There were no murders.

Most people on Adon had been alive for hundreds if not thousands of years. Like Adam, they were all aging and would eventually die.

"Flesh gives birth to flesh," Jesus said. "The spirit gives birth to spirit."

Nicholas twisted his lips to the side in confusion. "I don't understand."

A cool breeze was blowing.

"Do you feel the breeze?" Jesus asked.

"Yes."

"Do you know where it comes from?"

"No."

"Such are the things of the spirit. You can feel the breeze. You can even hear it sometimes. But you don't know where it comes from or where it's going. Such it is with everyone who is born of the spirit."

"How can this be? How can I be born of the spirit? I am my mother's son."

"You are also Adon's teacher. And yet you do not understand these things? I've spoken to you of simple things that even a child can understand."

"A child would never understand this."

"Unless you become like a child, you will never enter the kingdom of heaven."

"I am old. How can I become a child?"

The disciples were confused as well.

"I have spoken to you of worldly things. Yet you don't believe. How can you understand the things of the spirit unless your eyes are opened to see."

Nicholas was dumbfounded. He asked Jesus a number of questions, trying to trick him. Jesus had a comeback for each one. Nicholas tried to argue with him.

"You hypocrite," Jesus said angrily. "Why do you, being evil, try to trap me?"

"I'm not a hypocrite. I'm not evil. My sins are forgiven."

At that moment, a group of men brought to Jesus a paralytic man. They carried him on a stretcher.

Jesus saw their faith. "Be of good cheer," he said to the man on the pallet. "Your sins are forgiven."[6]

"Only God can forgive sins!" Nicholas said.

"I am the way, the truth and the life. No one comes to the Father but through me."[7]

"You are dishonoring God."

"Which is easier for me to say to the man? Your sins are forgiven, or take up your pallet and walk?"

Nicholas didn't answer.

"So that you know that I have power to forgive sins," Jesus turned to the man on the stretcher and said, "take up your pallet and go home."

The man suddenly stood to his feet. A crowd had followed the man and let out a collective gasp. Then a cheer.

Nicholas left angry. Adam could tell from his body language that he was not persuaded. How could he reject Christ after seeing such a miracle? It was beyond comprehension.

After he was gone and the crowd had dispersed, the disciples asked Jesus privately, "How can we become like a child?"

Everything that had happened that day had raised a number of questions in their minds. Jesus was more than willing to answer them.

"Whoever humbles himself like a child, is the one who will see the kingdom of heaven."[8]

That made sense to Adam. To be born again, didn't mean literally. But spiritually.

"Have you forgiven us of our sins?" Ethan asked.

"Yes. I came to take away the sins of the entire world."

"If all the sins of the world are forgiven, then how come you didn't forgive Nicholas of his sins?"

"I did."

"We don't understand," Lucas asked. "Does that mean he is saved? You called Nicholas a hypocrite. Aren't we all hypocrites?"

"There is one sin that God will not forgive."

"What's that?" Martin asked.

"Unbelief. If a man rejects the son, God will not forgive him of that sin. So he will die in all his sins. If a man believes in me, then God will remember his sins no more."

They were all amazed.

"If we're forgiven of our sins, why does it matter how much we sin?" Christopher asked.

"Don't let sin reign in your mortal bodies. Offer yourselves to God as an instrument of righteousness. Nicholas has let sin be his master. He is under the law of sin and death."[9]

"So we are different?" Abe asked.

"You are not under the law of sin and death, but under grace."

"What is grace?" Lucas asked.

"Grace is a free gift from God given to those who believe by faith."

"What is faith?"

"It's the substance of things hoped for. The evidence of things not seen. If you believe in me, then you will keep my commandments."[10]

"What is the most important commandment to keep?"

"Love the Lord your God with all your body, mind, and soul. And love your neighbor as yourself."[11]

"Well said, Jesus," Ethan said. "You're right. We should love God. We walked with him in the garden. We know how good he is."

"To love each other is more important than keeping the laws," Martin added.

They all agreed.

"You are not far off from the kingdom of heaven," Jesus replied.

One of the followers of Jesus suddenly appeared. He was out of breath. Like he'd been running.

"Nicholas went back to King Aza and told him what you said. He is planning to come and arrest all of you."

Jesus' brow was furrowed. His tone was serious. Not fearful but concerned.

"Adam, go to your spacecraft and gather all the seeds and packets of food," he said. "Take some of the disciples with you. Distribute the food to the poor in Center City."

All volunteered. Half stayed behind. The journey would be dangerous. They had to go through the center of the city to get to the spacecraft.

This took several days. They saw soldiers but they didn't approach them.

When they were done, they met Jesus back at Elias' house. Jesus instructed the disciples to have all their family and friends meet them there, packed, and ready to go to the eastern territory. Followers of Christ were no longer safe in the central district.

Jesus led the throng of people to the eastern district, providing them food and drink along the way.

Once they were several miles from the central district, the Lord sent a rain upon Adon for forty days and forty nights.

Not a flood like what had happened on Earth, but enough rain that a large body of water separated the central and eastern territories.

So Aza and his soldiers could not reach them.

15

Thirty years later

Adam lay on his back in a lush meadow, enjoying the afternoon sun. Half asleep. Elias called out his name. He sat up and saw his friend walking down the hill toward him.

"What are you doing out this way?" Adam asked.

"Looking for you. Why did you have to be so far away from the city? I had to walk all the way out here to find you."

Elias said it in a fake sharp and sarcastic tone. Clearly joking.

"I obviously didn't do a good enough job hiding, since you found me," Adam said with a grin.

Elias laughed and pulled Adam into a hug and kissed him on the cheek.

"Anytime you're looking for me, it means you want to put me to work," Adam joked.

"Not this time. Jesus wants to talk to you. He sent me to find you. I thought I might find you here. Since this is your favorite spot."

"Did he say what he wanted?" Adam asked.

"Didn't ask. He wants to talk to all of us."

Adam gathered his things, and they began walking back up the hill.

"Hey, you know what Sophie told me," Elias said with a mischievous gleam in his eyes.

"I don't think I want to know."

"Rachel has her eye on you. I have no idea why."

Adam pushed Elias playfully.

"Only one eye on me? What about her other eye? Is there something wrong with it?" Adam made a strange face distorting his eyes and mouth.

"You're one to talk. You only had one eye when I met you."

"Don't remind me. Anyway, not interested," Adam said emphatically. "It's better to be single. No offense to you and Sophie. How long have you been married now?"

"Over three thousand years?"

"I can't imagine it. You guys figured out how to make it work. I want to focus on serving God."

As they came over the hill, they saw a majestic city. Crystal buildings glistened with a perfectly blue sky as the background.

"So beautiful," Adam said.

At that moment, a tiger emerged from the woods and ran up to Adam with a ball in his mouth and rolled it in front of him.

Elias laughed. "Those tigers still like to play with you."

Adam tossed the ball. The tiger ran, picked it up in its mouth, and brought it back to Adam's feet. Adam threw it again, and the tiger brought it back again.

This went on for several minutes until Elias said, "We'd better go. We don't want to keep Jesus waiting."

On their several-mile walk back to the city, they passed a number of parks where children were playing. Several beautiful white churches stood along the way. Once a week, everyone gathered for fellowship and teaching.

Just ahead, Joshua came running toward them.

Joshua worked for Aza back in the central district. Before Aza was king. Joshua persecuted and had many of Jesus' followers killed. When Elias was stoned to death, the other soldiers laid their coats at his feet. An edict of the king said all executions had to be carried out by Joshua.

One day, while walking along a road, Jesus came up to him and said, "Joshua! Joshua! Why are you persecuting me?"[1]

"Who are you?" Joshua asked.

A bright light blinded him.

"I'm Jesus the one you are persecuting."

After spending several hours with Jesus, Joshua was converted, and Jesus healed his eyes. He began preaching that Jesus was indeed the Son of God.

When they all fled the central district thirty years before, Joshua came with them. At first, the disciples were wary of him. Now they loved him.

Seeing him running toward them warmed Adam's heart. They embraced warmly, and Adam and Elias kissed Joshua on both cheeks.

Joshua said to Elias, "I have some more writings for you to read. I want to get your input before I send them out to all the churches."

He'd been recording all of Jesus' writings and sayings and transcribing them, making them available to the churches. Jesus had made Joshua an apostle. Replacing Jeb. Under his leadership, churches had started all through the eastern district of Adon.

The area had become like a paradise. Not as beautiful and lush as the Garden of Eden but more like it every day.

When they first arrived, there was a drought and famine. The forty days and forty nights of rain ended the drought. When the rain ended, the people planted seeds. They multiplied, and within a year a harvest provided more than enough food for everyone. Every year they would harvest the crops and then have a big celebration.

Most of the animals fled Adon after the fall and had settled in that region. When the rains came, they all gathered on the hilltops until it stopped. When the multitude followed Jesus to the eastern district, the animals were reluctant at first to interact with them. Afraid of being hunted and killed, they mostly hid in the forests.

As sin began to diminish in the territory and man was no longer a danger to them, they became tame again. Most of the animals still remembered what it was like back before the fall and slowly warmed back up to man. Children played with wild animals again, and, for the most part, the people lived in harmony with the animals.

Sin still existed, but the people were quick to confess their sins to each other so they could be healed. Jesus taught them how to forgive just as he had forgiven them. Sicknesses still came upon them occasionally, but Jesus told them to go to the elders of the church and to let them anoint their heads with oil, and the prayer of faith would bring them healing.[2] He insisted they go to each other rather than to him for healing so they could take their own authority over sickness.

Disagreements were quickly resolved. If someone offended another, Jesus instructed him to go to that person and resolve it immediately. After thirty years, the people were starting to understand the grace of God and love for their fellow man. Consequently, there was no crime, no conflict, and they were slowly regaining what had been lost in the fall.

The eastern district became more beautiful every day. The streets were well maintained, the yards well-manicured. The houses weren't in disrepair, and neighbors helped each other when there was a need.

They all went from house to house eating, drinking, and worshiping God. Businesses were established, but no one charged for their services. If anyone had any need, someone stepped up and gave it to his brother or sister. No one had more than another. They had no need for money, and everyone loved God and loved each other.

The two greatest commandments.

Adam and Elias looked over Joshua's writings and approved. They reminded Adam of Paul's writings in the Bible.

They continued walking toward the magnificent crystal city.

"Look at that," Elias said, pointing west.

Adam looked to his right. The sky glistened off a large body of water. The Sea of Adon. When the forty-day rain came, it filled the valley with water, and became a separation between the eastern district and the central district still controlled by Aza.

The sea was a protective buffer for the people from King Aza. Aza had no way to get to Jesus, Adam, or any of his disciples. One of Jesus' disciples was a fisherman, and Jesus showed him how to build boats. Being a carpenter by trade.

On any given day, hundreds of boats and people were out on the lake fishing, boating, swimming, and playing. They were careful not to stray too close to the central district. Often, the villagers of the district would stand on the shore watching them.

Everyone felt bad for them. Aza's rule was bringing them tremendous suffering.

Adam, Elias, and Joshua made their way to a café where Jesus said to meet him. The same people who ran the café in Adon, where Adam first met Adam and Eve, ran this cafe.

Jesus and the other disciples were already there. The greetings were warm and friendly as the men hugged and kissed each other on the cheeks. The men had become very close friends, serving with each other and Jesus all those years. Everyone realized how fortunate they were to be on the eastern side of the sea away from the persecution.

Most importantly, they were with Jesus. The author and finisher of their faith.[3]

Adam figured this was a picture of what heaven would be like.

As Jesus stood to speak, the room grew quiet.

* * *

I looked out over the room at my disciples and leaders with great admiration. Of all my groups of twelve disciples from many worlds, these twelve were among the best. Faithful, dependable, trustworthy, loving, and they would follow me anywhere.

"I want to tell you some things, some mysteries," I said.

The disciples looked at me intently.

"God created many worlds like Earth, where Adam came from. He created Adon. Sin entered those worlds, just like it did to this one. I came to all of them and died as a sacrifice. I suffered many things."

I saw Adam grimace. Knowing he felt a pang in his heart. Even though he knew he was forgiven for eating the apple, it sometimes was still hard for him to believe.

"I came to destroy the work of the enemy in every world," I said. "My purpose for leaving heaven and coming to the planets was to restore what was lost in the Garden of Eden. To take the curses God had put on the people and place them upon myself."

I paused to let those words take effect.

Earth suddenly came to mind.

Such a waste.

Shortly after I was crucified on Earth, the church was formed and began to fulfill my vision. Not that many years later, they got away from my teachings. The Bible was held from the masses. The church began to accumulate riches. Evil men ruled the church.

The dark ages ensued. Such unnecessary suffering.

So many atrocities were committed in my name. As if people could be forced to believe in me.

Then God sent a great revival. A reformation. A renaissance. What followed was several centuries of innovation. More peaceful times.

The church exploded in growth. So many were added.

I desire that no man would perish, that all would have eternal life. I love everyone God created.

But the church on Earth changed. They began to fight among themselves. Splitting into many denominations. The unity of the church was disrupted. Nothing like what I had envisioned it to be.

The Holy Spirit had agreed to come and live in them and empower them. He was ignored. Rarely talked about in church. Miracles and healings became rare.

I told them the works that I did, they could do. Even more. The same power that raised me from the dead, lived inside of them.

But they were not seeking me.

For although they knew God, they neither glorified him as God nor gave thanks to him. Their foolish hearts were darkened. Their thinking became futile.

My Father gave them up to their shameful lusts.

They gave in to every kind of wickedness, evil, greed, and depravity. Full of envy, murder, strife, deceit, and malice.

Exchanging the natural for the unnatural.

They had no understanding, no love, no mercy.

They not only continued to do those things, but approved of those who practiced them. Those that knew me, were hardly different than those who didn't in how they lived.

It broke my heart.

Earth became so bad and the evil one so powerful, that God had to act. For the sake of the elect. Otherwise, everything would've been destroyed.

The other planets were virtually the same.

None of the worlds ever fully understood why I came. Even after I died, they continued to live in their fallen state and let sin abound. Grace abounded more, but God intended so much more for his people when he sent me to die for them.

My thoughts returned to the ones sitting in front of me. I had an important point I wanted to make to them.

"In the other worlds, God only permitted me to stay for three years, and then I had to die for the sins of the people."

"You have been with us for thirty years," Elias said.

Jesus nodded. "I asked God to let me stay in Adon longer so I could show you how to restore those things lost in the fall when God cursed Adon."

The disciples looked at each other and nodded in agreement as if they understood what I was saying.

I continued. "With your help, we've restored Adon to what I'd intended for all the other worlds. You've learned to live in harmony and love for each other and for God. What was lost in the fall is being restored."

"Amen. Amen."

"Now, it's time for me to go back to the central district."

16

Adam knew what was coming. He'd read the biblical accounts. Other than Jesus, he was the only one of the disciples who knew. Jesus had forbidden him to tell them.

It all made sense to him. Jesus would go to the central district and offer himself up as a sacrifice for the sins of everyone on Adon.

"I can't ignore the cries of my people in the central district," Jesus said to the disciples. "I hear their suffering under the hand of Aza. I must go and deliver them."

Jesus sat down.

Adam didn't know everything, but he knew a lot. The disciples wouldn't understand what the word "deliver" meant. They were naïve. They didn't believe that Aza could do anything to Jesus.

That's why they didn't offer any resistance when Jesus said he was going there. Years before, they might've argued that it was too dangerous. After spending thirty years with Jesus, they believed he was indestructible. They'd seen him raise Elias from the dead. They'd seen him perform many miracles.

In reality, they mistakenly believed that Jesus was going to the central district to overthrow Aza and set the people free. Rather than being fearful, they were excited.

Liam, the soldier, was itching to go.

They didn't understand that Jesus wasn't going to the central district to overthrow Aza, but to turn himself in.

To die.

Why?

Because it was the only way. Man was a sinner. All had sinned and fallen short of the glory of God.[1] Sin had to be punished. God demanded it.

Man can do nothing to atone for his sin. Because of that, man could never enter into the presence of God.

If someone could live his or her entire life without sin, then he or she could get into heaven. But that's impossible. Jesus was the only one who could live a perfect life without sin.

Looking at it from this perspective, there was no hope for man. But Jesus took man's punishment upon himself. On Earth, God poured out all his wrath onto his son, Jesus.

He was about to do the same thing on Adon.

"I am going back to Adon with you," Adam said. "There's something I must face."

Jesus nodded. He knew what Adam meant.

All the disciples said, "We will go as well."

Jesus stood up again and said, "We'll go to Adon and set my people free. Don't be afraid."

"We aren't afraid."

Joshua said, "I'll go, too."

Jesus shook his head. "No, Joshua. Stay here for now. I have called you to Adon to spread my gospel. Keep writing. Send letters to the churches explaining the things I've shown you. God has given you the privilege and authority as an apostle to tell everyone what God has done for them so they will believe in me and bring glory to God's name."

By the look on his face, Joshua seemed disappointed, but didn't offer any resistance.

Jesus said, "Elias you stay here as well."

"I want to go with you," Elias said.

"No, stay here with your family. You've already been martyred once for me. Your rewards in heaven will be great. Upon this rock, I will build my church."

If Elias was disappointed, he didn't say.

Jesus said to the other disciples, "Follow me." He walked down to the edge of the sea where a boat was waiting.

"Go and say goodbye to your families and meet me back here," he said. "Go quickly."

A few minutes later, they gathered by the sea along with a huge throng to see them off. After many tearful goodbyes, one by one they all got on the boat. Adam wondered if they would ever be back there again.

Jesus said, "I'll meet you on the other side."

He started walking away. Two of the disciples shoved the boat into the sea, and they started rowing to Adon.

After they were away from the shore, Adam looked at the other disciples with admiration. He had grown very close to them. They were all different. They came from different backgrounds, and all had different strengths and weaknesses. The one common bond was that they all loved Jesus.

They didn't seem afraid. These men were solid. None of them would betray or deny Jesus. They wouldn't flee at the sight of soldiers. They had thirty plus years with Jesus and were willing to lay down their lives for him.

Even if they didn't think it'd be necessary.

The boat was a considerable distance from the land when the winds began to buffet it. They were terrified.

Adam could feel his heart pounding in his chest.

He clutched the side of the boat so hard that his knuckles were white. He wasn't sure why it hadn't already capsized. They were taking on water. The men were desperately trying to get the water out of the boat. They didn't have anything to scoop it out. They had to do it with their hands.

It felt hopeless.

Adam didn't think this was how they were going to die, but he wasn't certain of it.

The storm continued through the night. Never letting up. They gave up rowing. The winds were too strong. When they subsided for a short period of time, they tried to row with the wind back toward the eastern district, but the winds ripped the oars out of their hands and into the sea.

They were totally at the mercy of the wind and sea. Everyone slumped down in the boat and held on for dear life.

To make matters worse, it was pitch black around them. Illuminated only between lightning strikes. They were wet, tired, and cold. With no idea how far away from the land they were. If the boat did capsize, Adam had no idea which direction to swim.

At least they were still alive.

Shortly before dawn they saw a figure off in the distance. A white glow in the shape of a man wearing a white robe. His face was glowing, brightening the sky.

"It's Jesus!" Ethan said, when the image got closer.

"It can't be. He's not in a boat. He's walking on water."[3]

"It's a ghost," one of them cried out in fear.

The winds intensified. The boat rocked violently from side to side. It felt like it could splinter apart at any minute.

Adam was afraid but remembered the account in the Bible. How Jesus walked on water in similar circumstances. Calmed the storm. He also remembered what Peter did.

Should I?

Did I dare ask?

He somehow found the courage. Especially after he heard Jesus' voice.

"Take courage," Jesus said. "It is I. Don't be afraid."

The other disciples cried out to him. "Save us, Jesus. The boat is about to sink."

"Lord, if it's you," Adam said, "tell me to come to you on the water."

Adam moved closer to the front of the boat. Lifted his leg like he was about to go overboard. Didn't even hesitate. If he thought about it too long, he would've chickened out.

"Are you crazy?"

"You've lost your mind."

"You'll drown."

"Come," Adam heard Jesus say.

He felt this overwhelming faith come over him. As soon as he climbed out of the boat, the wind died down. The waves were high, but Adam started walking toward Jesus. Jesus reached out and took Adam's hand. They began walking together.

The sun appeared. The waves completely subsided at Jesus' command.

An unspeakable joy came over Adam.

I'm walking on water!

He remembered how Peter became afraid and began to sink. Those negative thoughts crept into his mind. He tamped them out. Clutched Jesus' hand even tighter.

Without warning, Jesus let go of his hand. Adam let out a screech. To his amazement, he didn't sink. He was still able to walk on the water. He began running and leaping. Dancing with joy. Bouncing around like a little kid.

All the disciples said, "We want to walk on water too!"

Jesus said, "Come on. You can all come to me."

One by one, the disciples got out of the boat, and all began walking to Jesus. They jumped and played outside the boat for more than ten minutes.

When they were all back in the boat, Jesus said, "You are men of such great faith. I tell you this, I haven't seen such great faith anywhere in the universe."

A gentle breeze pushed them toward the central district shoreline. Good thing since they didn't have any way to propel the boat in that direction. On the way, Jesus instructed them on what would happen in Adon. Adam figured Jesus commanded the wind to blow in that direction.

As they neared the shore, a large crowd awaited their arrival. The people had seen them coming from a distance and recognized Jesus at once. The word spread that Jesus was back. They went throughout the countryside to bring everyone they knew to see the great healer.

Jesus didn't disappoint. He healed all who were sick. Preached the good news for hours.

When he was finished teaching, he set his face to walk to the city and the people followed. Praising and worshiping him along the way. One person had a donkey for him to ride.

As they approached the city, Jesus looked over it and wept.[4]

* * *

The crowd formed a procession, and all the people were praising me. My heart was warmed as they were glad to see me. I was glad to see them as well. While I enjoyed the thirty years in the eastern district, I couldn't stop thinking about my children here who needed me. Their suffering had been great, and I'd heard their cries. My time hadn't yet come, or I would've come sooner.

Most think I'd come to overthrow the king. They didn't understand why I had to come and die. My kingdom will be established, but not on Adon. It'll be an eternal kingdom. One that's not perishable and will last forever.

In Heaven.

When my work was finished on Adon, I'd go and finish preparing the mansions for those who believed in me.

The people were shouting, "Praise to King Jesus." I love the praises of the people. I inhabit them. If they didn't worship me, the stones would cry out.

Many were weak, sick, and dying prematurely. I healed them all. Many were downcast. I brought them hope.

Several members of the High Council were in the crowd. I instructed them to go back to the palace and tell Aza I would come to him tomorrow morning at first light.

Aza was on my mind. He would have a restless night. He'd be worried that I've come back to take his kingdom from him. I wish he'd repent. I'll give him that chance in the morning. God always gives every man a chance to turn from his ways. Sadly, Aza will harden his heart like his father before him.

I turned my attention back to the crowd and spoke to them.

"In a little while, you will no longer see me. I've come into the world having left my Father. I'm leaving the world again and going to my Father. But I will come to you again."[5]

The crowd murmured. They didn't understand what I was saying.

"Go back to your homes. Meet me at the shores of the sea in three days. Tell everyone."

The people didn't want to leave, but darkness had come upon Adon, and everyone scattered to their own homes. The disciples were still there with me. We formed a circle and sat down together. Earlier, I had instructed one of the disciples to find some bread and wine.

This was one of my favorite things to do.

"Whoever eats my flesh and drinks my blood has eternal life," I said.[6]

My disciples had the weirdest looks on their faces. I knew what they were thinking. How could they eat my flesh and drink my blood?

I would reveal all these truths and more to Joshua. After I'm gone. So he can write them down in letters to the churches. The gospel will seem difficult to understand for some. It shouldn't be. It's simple.

For by grace all men are saved through faith. Not of themselves so they could not boast. Believe in me and confess me as Lord and they will be saved.[7]

They don't have to do the work. I will do it for them.

While we reclined at the table, I said to them, "I have eagerly desired to eat this supper with you before I suffer."

They began to talk at once.

"What do you mean by suffer, Jesus?"

They'd know soon enough. For tonight, I wanted to enjoy this time with them.

"One day, we will all be dining together in heaven at the marriage supper of the Lamb. I look forward to that day."

"So do we."

I smiled.

How could they possibly know what awaited us tomorrow?

17

I took the bread and broke it. Giving thanks, I looked up to heaven and blessed it. As was my custom. The disciples knew that. They'd seen me bless the food for thirty years. I had instructed them to do the same.

"This is my body that's broken for you," I said. "As often as you eat of this bread, do it in remembrance of me."[1]

Each disciple took a piece of bread, and we ate together. I explained how my body had to be broken for the sicknesses of the world.

When sin came into a world, it brought with it sickness and sorrows. It was up to me to carry all the consequences of sin. Spiritually and physically.

I poured the wine into a cup, passed it around, and we all drank together.

"This is my blood that's shed for you. As often as you drink from this cup, do it in remembrance of me."

I explained how my blood would be shed for the sins of the world, covering them with an eternal sacrifice. Except for the unpardonable sin. The sin of unbelief. Rejecting me.

"Unless you eat the flesh of the Son of Man and drink his blood, you have no life in you. Whoever eats my flesh and drinks my blood has eternal life, I will raise them up at the last day."

We finished the rest of the bread and wine until everyone was satisfied. For four hours, I explained many things to them. We'd had a long day and they were getting tired.

"I'm only with you a little while longer. Where I'm going, you cannot come. I give you one last command: Love one another, as I have loved you. They'll know you're my disciples by your love for one another."[2]

They all stood and embraced each other. My heart warmed as I watched them. I prayed the Father would keep them safe.

"Go back to Elias' house," I said. "Do not leave there. Stay for three days, and then meet me at the sea the morning of the third day."

They all started to leave.

"Adam, stay with me," I said.

"I want to stay with you," Ethan said emphatically. The others agreed.

"What I must do, I must do alone. I want to talk to Adam first," I explained.

They were all sad but reluctantly left as I had commanded.

I sent them off with this word, "You have sorrow now, but I'll see you again. Then your hearts will rejoice, and no one will be able to take your joy away from you."[3]

I hugged them all, kissed them on the cheeks, and sent them on their way.

Adam and I left and went over the ravine and down to the Garden of Sorrows. We went deep into the garden to the exact spot where Adam had eaten from the tree of the knowledge of good and evil.

We sat down next to a rock where the tree once stood.

It doesn't get any easier.

I had given my life many times. The next three days were going to be hard.

"Adam, my soul is deeply grieved to the point of death. Will you remain here with me?"[4]

"Of course, I will, Lord." Adam said with deep conviction.

I began praying fervently.

Adam was sleepy but refused to go to sleep. He stayed awake with me the entire time. It brought me great comfort knowing he was there.

"Lord, may I ask you a question?" Adam asked. I looked up from praying and nodded.

"So many things have happened here on Adon that are similar to what happened on earth. Why is that? This is a whole different planet. Yet the same things I read about in the Bible keep happening here. Turning the water into wine, raising Elias from the dead, walking on water. Now we're here at the garden, the night before your death just like in the Bible."

"God is the same yesterday, today, and forever. His words never change,"[5] I explained.

"What about the woman who touched your garment in Gomor? She said the same thing the woman on earth said, 'If I can just touch his garment I will be healed.'"

"There's nothing new under the sun.[6] The Holy Spirit is the same here as he was on Earth. He's the one who told her to touch my garment, and if she did, she would be healed. That's what he told the woman with the issue of blood on earth. They both had to respond in faith."

Adam nodded his head as if he finally understood.

For several hours, I explained many of the mysteries of heaven and earth. I told him how the events on all the planets were very similar. Even in the solemnity of the moment, we laughed several times as we talked about Adam's journey from Earth to Adon. Adam gave me great comfort in my time of need.

At one point, Adam got a serious look on his face.

"Lord, what's it like for you?"

I knew what he was asking.

I hesitated. Then I felt a release. God gave me permission to share my innermost thoughts.

"The physical pain is excruciating," I began. "However, the spiritual pain is what causes the greatest agony and anguish."

Adam listened intently, paying close attention to each word.

"Everything always happens in the same order. The circumstances aren't always the same. The manner of death is always different. But ... the end result is always the same."

"When I first stand before the ruler is when I take the shame of the world upon myself."

I let those words sink in.

Adam took my hand.

"The taunts ... Men ridicule me. Mock me. Revile me."

Adam squeezed my hand harder.

"They always speak lies about me. Say things that aren't true. I always remain silent during this time. No matter what they say, I stay quiet. I don't answer them. On Earth, they put a crown of thorns on my head. The pain was intense as they pressed the thorns deep into my forehead. They hit me in the face. Spit on me. Slap me. I never respond. I just take it."

I stopped to take in a deep breath. My voice was quivering. I'm fully God. Yet, at these moments, I feel my humanity. It's part of God's brilliant plan. I must be tempted in every way, just like man. I must feel what he feels. The shame is on me, like it is on them.

It's the only way.

"The shame ... the guilt ... the condemnation. I feel the humiliation. It's not my shame; it's everyone's. I know how you feel Adam about eating the fruit. I felt what you felt at that moment. My heart breaks for you. I asked my Father to take it away from you and let me bear it, so you don't have to. Everyone's shame is on me at the same time."

Adam began to cry. He looked around. Where the rivers once flowed were nothing but creek beds. The stones no longer like jewels. No evidence the tree of the knowledge of good and evil had ever stood there. Obviously remembering.

When he regained his composure, Adam said, "I still feel it. Right here on this spot. I brought sin into the world. I still sin. What I want to do, I don't. What I don't want to do, I still do. I still feel the guilt."[7]

"God knows that, Adam. He knows the shame you feel when you sin. That's why I come to these worlds. To take that shame. To take your guilt."

"You've done nothing to deserve it. What do you have to be ashamed of?"

"It's a free gift. Accept it."

Adam seemed to understand. I continued.

"After I have taken the shame, I must take the sicknesses and diseases."

"The stripes," Adam said.

I nodded.

"There are always stripes. There must be so my children can be healed. Thirty-nine of them. Every time ... every world ... Always thirty-nine. It's my burden to bear."

Adam put his hand on my shoulder. Stroked my back knowing that was where I would take the stripes. I cringed slightly when he touched my back.

"It must be horrible," he said.

"I count the stripes. Every one of them. I must take them."

"You are so brave. I don't know how you do it." Adam trembled, his body tense, drawn almost into a fetal position. I wondered if I was sharing too much.

"With each stripe, more sicknesses and diseases are put upon me. The whips rip my flesh, but the pain tears at my heart and soul. I feel the suffering. Everyone's. Adam, I've never been sick a day in my life. Suddenly, every sickness and disease are upon me, ravaging my body. I feel the same things my children feel, except it's all at once. Everybody's suffering is on me like a large boulder pressing against my chest. I can feel the strain on my heart as it struggles to maintain each beat. I want to die. I can't. I must stay alive long enough to take the sins upon myself. It's as much as one man can bear … But I have to find the strength."

"I can't imagine."

"That's not the worst part."

"The sins," Adam said.

I nod as the anguish and agony flood every fiber of my being.

"My manner of death is different on each planet. What's always the same is that the sins are placed upon me right before I die. Then…"

My voice cracks. I can't continue. Tears run down my face.

Adam reached to wipe them away. He looked at his hand. Blood … I'm sweating drops of blood.[8]

"Then what?" Adam said in a soft, gentle voice.

Then God forsakes me.

I try to speak the words but can't.

Pain. Anguish. Agony…I can feel it already as if it's happening right now.

"God can't even look at me."

"I've been with God since the foundation of the world. My Father and I are one. When the sins of the world come upon me, he abandons me. I'm all alone. The punishment of the world is upon me."

"I'm so sorry." Adam wept.

"That's why there is darkness. God can't even look at me."

I take a deep breath.

"On Earth, you asked God to take the cup from you," Adam said, choking back the sobs. "Will you do that now?"

"No. I only asked that one time. He would not take the cup from me. It had to be my choice."

"Ask him now. Maybe he would this time."

"Don't you know that I could call down ten thousand angels at any time and God would rescue me?"

"I know."

At that moment, an angel appeared to me and strengthened me. The resolve in my voice returned.

"Not my will, but yours be done," I said to my Father.

"That's why I came," I said to Adam. "It's why you're not condemned. Everyone can have eternal life because of my sacrifice."

"Thank you so much. Words cannot even express ..." Adam's voice trailed off.

I embraced Adam. We held the embrace for several seconds. I want him to feel my love for him.

The clock turned to three. The fourth watch.

Time for me to pray.

"Adam, you must leave now. I must go to Aza at the first light."

"I want to stay with you," Adam implored.

"You can't. They'll kill you too, and your time has not yet come. Remember what I said about how God is going to use you to save the people. That time is near."

I stood and placed my hands on Adam's shoulders. I looked him squarely in the eyes.

"Go back to the house. Get some rest. Pray for me. In three days, I'll rise from the dead and my work will be done. Tell the disciples to meet at the sea three days from now in the morning. Don't leave the house. Soldiers will be looking for all of you."

Adam wrapped his arms around me and squeezed hard. It felt good.

He has come so far ...

18

Adam went to Elias' house where the disciples were sleeping. He prayed for several minutes and then fell asleep himself.

Lucas woke him. "Where is Jesus?"

"He went to the palace to face Aza."

"You let him go alone?"

"He wouldn't let me go with him."

"We need to wake the others and go be with him."

Lucas started to go and wake them, but Adam stopped him.

"I wanted to go with him. He wouldn't let me. We need to stay in the house. It's safe here. If we go out, Aza will have us killed. Jesus said it's something he must do alone."

Lucas seemed to understand. Adam and Lucas stayed up talking, and Adam explained the things Jesus had said to him the night before.

Adam kept looking at the clock. He knew what Jesus was going through. He tried to envision what was happening and when.

How will Aza kill him?

Lucas tried to console Adam but couldn't.

The earthquake. . . Darkness. They would signal the end.

It was all his fault.

Suddenly, a violent quake, and darkness came over Adon as if it were night. Adam was surprised it'd happened so quickly. A sense of relief came over him.

Thank you, God, he didn't have to suffer long.

The other disciples ran into the room.

"What happened?" they asked.

Adam knew. His hands started shaking. He wanted to speak but was so choked up the words wouldn't come.

"Jesus...He's..." Adam's voice cracked. "Dead." Adam buried his head in his hands.

"He's dead?" Liam asked. "How do you know? What happened to him? I thought he was with you. Did you leave him alone? He can't be dead. He told us to meet him back here."

"No," Zach said excitedly. "He told us to come back here and to stay for three days. He never said he was going to meet us here."

"He said he'd meet us in three days at the sea," Lucas said. "We are supposed to tell everyone."

"How can he meet us if he's dead?"

"I don't believe he's dead," Abe said. "Not unless I see it with my own eyes."

The disciples talked among themselves for several minutes contemplating the turn of events. Jesus said he was going to suffer, but they didn't know he was going to die.

Adam felt new resolve come over him. Jesus wouldn't want him to be sad. The words started to make sense.

"Jesus knew Aza would kill him," Adam told them. "That's why he came back to Center City. I was with him last night at the Garden of Sorrows. I didn't leave him. He sent me away. He told me to come back to the house and stay with you. We are to stay here and meet him at the Sea of Adon in three days."

"Why would they kill Jesus? What was the charge?" Liam said angrily.

"They must've said that Jesus ate the apple in the garden. I saw a sign with a warrant out for his arrest on the way over here." Zach said.

"There's no way Jesus ate the apple. That's a bogus charge," Ethan said emphatically. They all agreed.

Adam lowered his head extremely distressed.

Zach said, "What Adam?"

"I have something I need to tell all of you." Adam hesitated.

"What do you need to tell us, Adam?" Liam said in an accusatory tone.

"I'm the one who ate the apple."

He felt like the weight of the world had been lifted off his shoulders.

"*You* ate the apple!" Liam lunged to strike Adam, but Lucas stopped him.

"All this time it was you, and you never told us," Liam spat out.

"Calm down, Liam," Lucas said.

"Jesus died because of him."

"Jesus died for all our sins as much as he died for Adam's sin," Lucas said.

"Liam is right," Tobi said, his voice loud and angry. "You need to leave, Adam. We don't want you here. You have no right to come here now and try to be one of us. Adam and Eve are dead because of you. Our lives were great before you came along."

The words pierced Adam's heart. He felt the shame all over again.

Martin walked over to his brother, Tobi, and put his hand on his shoulder to calm him. "Everybody needs to calm down. Jesus told us to love each other at all times no matter what we have done."

He turned to Adam, "Did Jesus know you're the one who ate the apple?"

"Yes." Adam could barely respond.

"What did he say?"

"He told me he...he did not condemn me." Saying the words aloud gave them new meaning.

"How long has Jesus known?" Lucas asked.

"Since the beginning."

Liam paced around. "He's not even one of us," Liam said angrily, pointing his finger at Adam. "He's from Earth. We're the ones Jesus called to be disciples. I say we kick him out of the house. Let him fend for himself. Aza's probably sending someone over here for him right now. They're going to arrest all of us because of him."

"I will just leave," Adam said as tears welled up in his eyes. The full force of the accusations and rejection hurt his heart.

"No, Adam," Martin said. "You're going to stay. We're all in this together. Jesus chose you as a disciple even though he knew you ate the apple. You're one of us. I know you. We've been with you for thirty years. You've stood by Jesus and us all this time. Whatever mistakes you made, you've more than made up for them."

"I agree with Martin," Lucas said. "Jesus told you to come back here and stay with us. If Jesus doesn't condemn you, we shouldn't either. Remember, Jesus said not to judge one another."

Martin walked over and put his arm around Adam and comforted him.

A loud knock on the door interrupted them. Everyone jumped.
Who could that be?

Zach went to look and see who it was. A member of the High Council named Jason, who had become a secret follower of Christ, was at the door. Zach let him in and locked the door behind him.

Jason immediately said, "Jesus is dead."

"We know. Adam was just telling us," Tobi said. "What happened?"

"The High Council met most of the night. The plan was to go and arrest Jesus, but no one knew where he was. While we were talking, he walked right in. Everyone was shocked to see him. He'd said he was going to come at first light, but no one believed it."

"What happened next?" Adam asked.

"Aza cowered behind one of his soldiers. He thought Jesus had come to kill him. Jesus just calmly said, 'Aza, I have come to tell you to let all my people go.'"

Jason stopped to catch his breath. Then he told them the whole story.

When Aza saw Jesus was unarmed and alone, he ordered the soldiers to seize him. Jesus didn't resist. The members of the High Council started accusing Jesus of many crimes. At first, Jesus didn't say a word.

Aza asked, "Were you the one who ate the apple in the garden?"

Jesus was silent. Didn't say a word.

"Aren't you going to answer them?" a member of the council asked. "What about all these charges we bring against you?"

A leading priest of the temple spoke up and said, "How could he have eaten the apple? He wasn't even born yet."

Liam interrupted Jason's account. "That's true. Jesus was born after Adam ate the apple. He couldn't have done it."

Jason started to speak, but then caught himself, obviously surprised by the new information that Adam had eaten the apple.

He looked at Adam. "After that, Aza started accusing Adam and said that Jesus was covering for you."

"What did he say?" Adam asked.

Jason related what had happened. "Aza said, 'The man from Earth ate the apple. Jesus has been hiding him from facing his punishment.'"

Aza asked Jesus, "Did Adam eat the apple?"

Jesus didn't answer.

Then Aza changed the subject and asked Jesus, "Are you a king?"

Jesus did answer. "You have said it."

Aza started shouting hysterically.

"You've set up a kingdom on the other side of the great lake. You've made yourself the king, and the people worship you."

Aza stepped out from behind where he was standing and stood in the center of the council closer to where Jesus was standing. He pointed accusingly at Jesus.

"What more proof do you need? He claims to be a king and has come to overthrow our government and set himself up as king. He must die."

Jesus said to the entire council, "My kingdom is not an earthly kingdom. If it were, my followers would fight to keep me from being handed over to you."

"So, you are a king. Who are your followers?" Aza said accusingly.

"You say I'm a king," Jesus answered. "Actually, I was born and came into the world to testify to the truth. All who love the truth recognize what I say is true. I've come to lead the people back to the eastern district where they can live free from your rule and in peace."

"There you heard it from his own mouth," a member of the council shouted out. "There's no king but Aza. This man has come to lead the people in an insurrection. I say he should be beheaded."

Another council member shouted, "Jesus should be whipped and then beheaded."

They agreed to have him whipped and then brought back to them.

They took Jesus away and brutally beat him. The soldiers mocked him and struck him in the face. His face was unrecognizable.

"They began beating him. He was tied to a post in the square." Jason's speech slowed and became deliberate as he related the account, his voice cracking, tears welling up in his eyes.

Thirty-nine lashes.

But the soldier missed one. He only hit Jesus with thirty-eight. Men untied Jesus from the post, but he refused to leave. He said that he had to take one more stripe. If he didn't some wouldn't be healed.

Four men tried to pull Jesus' arms off the post, but they couldn't. Jesus was so strong, even having been beaten and having lost so much blood. The soldier became angry. He hit Jesus with another stripe, but then wouldn't stop. He was so angry. His eyes filled with hate.

He hit Jesus thirty-nine more times after the one. No flesh was left on his back. People said they could see his internal organs through the muscle and tissue.

I don't know how he endured it.

They led Jesus back to the High Council, but Jesus fell on the way. He couldn't walk, so they carried him.

Several of the disciples wiped away tears that fell unbidden down their disheartened faces.

"The council members thought Jesus was dead, but Jesus lifted His head and said, "Father forgive them, for they know not what they do."[1]

The members of the council around me were stunned by his words.

"It is finished. Father, into your hands I commit my Spirit,"[2] Jesus said.

Then he died.

A soldier stuck a spear in Jesus's left side to see if he was dead. The quake hit, and everything went dark outside.

"Where is Jesus now?" Lucas said.

"Do you remember where Elias was buried before Jesus raised him from the dead?"

They all answered yes.

"That same man buried Jesus in the same tomb. He took a risk and asked Aza for the body. Aza said yes because he didn't want it near him in case someone tried to come for it. They wrapped Jesus' body in a cloth and took it to the tomb. Several of the ladies are preparing it for burial. Aza sent several guards to watch over it in case anyone tried to come and steal the body."

"Let's go there," Liam said.

"No," Adam responded. "Jesus said for us to stay here for three days and then meet him at the shore."

"I want to see for myself that he's really dead."

"He's dead, but he'll be raised on the third day. You just have to believe," Adam said.

"I do believe, but it's hard."

Adam placed his arm on Liam's shoulder and said, "Remember what Jesus said, 'Blessed are those who've not seen and yet believe.'"[3]

19

Three days later

King Aza had his soldiers search for the disciples and Adam for three days but couldn't find them. He assumed they went back across the lake. Jesus was dead, which pleased him, but he really wanted to kill Adam.

He could hardly believe it when one of his top deputies burst into his room and said, 'Jesus' body is missing! The stone is rolled away in front of the tomb, and the only thing left are his burial clothes."

"What about the guards? Where were they?" Aza said. Rage burned so strongly in him he couldn't see straight.

"They're nowhere to be found. We don't know what happened to them. Some of his followers said Jesus told everyone he would be raised from the dead in three days."

"It's a hoax," King Aza said. "They've stolen his body to make it look like he was resurrected so the people will follow him. Find the guards and kill them when you find them."

About that time another member of his staff rushed in. "All the people are gathering at the sea. Word's spreading that Jesus was raised from the dead and is going to meet them there."

"Gather up all of my armies and chariots," Aza said. "I want every soldier to meet me there in three hours. I'm going to defeat Jesus and his followers once and for all."

Aza turned to his top deputy. "Quick," he said. "We must hurry. I want to get to the sea before the disciples get away."

* * *

Early in the morning on the third day, the disciples and Adam were sitting at the table having a breakfast meal. Afterwards, they were going to leave for the sea. Liam had apologized to Adam privately and in front of everyone.

Tobi apologized as well. He went to Adam and told him he loved him like a brother. He felt bad he had made him feel worse.

Adam accepted their apologies and asked everyone to forgive him for eating the apple, which they all did readily.

Suddenly, a rushing wind filled the room.

Jesus was standing there among them!

Adam knew it was Jesus. He was overjoyed to see him. He stood right up from his chair and ran to him, hesitating at first to touch him. When Jesus opened his arms, Adam fell into them rejoicing to be with Jesus again.

At first, the disciples thought they were seeing a ghost. Jesus rebuked them for their unbelief.

As he spoke, they knew it was him. He showed them the wound on his side and the stripes on his back. They were filled with joy. Laughter filled the place as the sorrow had lasted through the night, but the joy had come in the morning.[1]

Jesus sat down and ate breakfast with them.

Afterward, he told them what was going to happen next, "All the people are gathering by the sea. You must go down and meet them.

I'll be there shortly. I am sending the Holy Spirit to live inside each of you."

He stretched out his hand and said, "Receive the Holy Spirit. You'll receive power and will be my witnesses throughout the world."[2]

Just like that, he was gone.

The disciples rushed to the sea, empowered by the Holy Spirit.

A throng of people were standing along the banks. Adam thought almost everyone from the central district was there. Adam felt the power of the Holy Spirit inside of him. Unlike anything he'd ever felt before.

He went to the front of the crowd, stood on a rock, and said, "People of Adon, listen to me. God has raised Jesus from the dead. We saw Jesus with our own eyes just a few minutes ago. Jesus told us to meet him here. He'll be here shortly."

A cheer went up from the crowd.

Adam had been afraid to speak in front of a small crowd on Earth. *If Courtney and Jamie could see me now.*

Liam stood and said, "Jesus is alive, and he's the Messiah!"

The crowd was in a frenzy. Many believed the disciples. Just as many were skeptical. All were anticipating that something big was about to happen. A buzz was flowing through the crowd like a wave.

Zach stood up and said, "Each of you must repent of your sins and turn to God. If you confess him as Lord and believe God has raised Jesus from the dead, you will be saved."[3]

The disciples took turns preaching for a long time, urging the people to believe in Jesus and the truth of his resurrection.

A roar went up from the crowd. People started pointing, jumping up and down, shouting. The disciples had their backs to the water. They turned to look.

Jesus appeared, walking on the water toward them. The crowd erupted in shouts of praise. "Blessed be the name of the Lord!" they proclaimed as Jesus walked all the way to the land.

Adam turned to the crowd raising his hands to silence them. "Do you finally believe?"

The crowd shouted, "Yes, we believe! We believe!"

Screams began coming from the people in the back. Adam looked that way and discovered Aza had assembled a large army headed right for them. A large plume of dust trailed them, revealing that the size of the army was massive.

The people panicked when they saw his army close to overtaking them. They started pushing closer to the sea.

They cried out to Jesus, "Did you bring us out here to die? We would rather be poor in Adon than dead here by the sea."

"Don't be afraid," Jesus said. "Just stand and watch God rescue you today. You'll never see Aza and his army again after today."[4]

The closer Aza got to the people, the more they began to panic. They were crowding closer to the shore and at risk of trampling each other.

Adam looked at Jesus and said, "Lord, we have to do something."

Jesus looked at Adam and said, "Remember what I said to you? That God would use you to save the people?"

Adam shook his head yes.

"You know what to do," Jesus said. "You've read how I rescued the people from Egypt."

"You want *me* to do it?" Adam asked, "I don't have enough faith."

"Do what?" Liam asked. "What do you want Adam to do?"

"Come on, Lord. You must do it," Adam implored Jesus.

"You have enough faith," Jesus said. "If you have faith the size of a mustard seed, you can say to the mountain move.[5] You can say to a sea to open, and it will. The same power that raised me from the dead is living inside of you. You'll not have me for much longer. It's time for you to use your faith. Adam, it's up to you."

"I'll see you on the other side," Jesus said.

With those final words, Jesus stepped back on the water and walked away until he was out of sight.

The disciples looked at Adam and then they looked back at Aza's armies rapidly approaching. The people were screaming frantically, crying out for someone to do something.

"Adam," Ethan said, "do whatever Jesus wants you to do. But do it now! We're running out of time!"

Adam turned to the sea and began walking toward it.

The disciples had a glazed look in their eyes, clueless as to what to do. The people were pushing and shoving and trying not to be the ones who Aza and his men came upon first.

Adam knew what Jesus wanted him to do. He'd read the biblical account of Moses parting the water and the people being saved. Would the water part for him? All these men, women, and children were counting on him.

What if I'm wrong?

But what if I'm right and that's what Jesus wants me to do?

Do I have the faith?

Adam stretched out his hand and put his foot in the water and began to wade out into the sea. Emboldened, he turned around and said to the other disciples, "Follow me."

"What are you doing?" Liam said. "Are all these people supposed to walk on water all the way to the other side?"

"Just watch what God is going to do," Adam said with more conviction than he was feeling inside. "Step out on faith and step into the water with me. We will see the hand of God deliver all the people."

Lucas stepped into the water first. The others followed. Adam motioned for everyone to wade into the water.

Reluctant at first, one by one, they waded into the water.

A mighty wind began to blow from the east. The sea parted and the water stood on both sides, turning the seabed into dry land.[6]

Adam stared at amazement at the wall of water on each side of the pathway. It's one thing to read about it in the Bible; another to be standing right there looking at tens of thousands of tons of water obeying his command.

But they didn't have much time to enjoy the sight. Adam stood at the entrance and called for the people to walk through the dry land and not stop until they got to the other side. The disciples stayed back helping those in need and encouraging everyone to keep moving. They seemed as stunned as Adam but were aware of the sense of urgency and the danger fast approaching.

Aza and his men had quickened their pace. Adam saw the horses, chariots, and soldiers stop when they got to the sea. They hesitated when they saw the wall of water on each side of them.

That made all the difference. The slight delay was all Adam needed to get everyone to the other side before Aza and his men could catch up to them.

When Aza finally got his men to follow, the people were nearing the other side. Adam calmly walked at the back of the crowd, making sure everyone got there safely and no one was left behind.

A multitude of people from the eastern district had gathered on the other side to see what was happening. Jesus stood there with them.

When Adam exited the sea, Aza and his men were only a hundred yards behind him. The hoof beat of the horses and Aza's cursing echoed off the sides of the water.

"I'm going to kill you! You are mine!" Aza shouted.

Jesus told Adam to raise his hand again and command the sea to return to its usual place.

Adam stretched out his hands. Aza was close enough that he could see his eyes.

Adam commanded the waters to return to their usual place. The sea roiled and began to cascade down with violent force.

Aza and his men screamed in horror as the water surrounded and then consumed them until they disappeared. The entire army drowned.

Not a single one survived. Their bodies were spit out of the sea onto the dry land on the other shore.

That was how the Lord rescued the people of Adon and brought them to the other side.

20

Joy and celebration spread throughout the land. Families and friends were reunited. The people in the eastern and central districts had not seen each other for thirty years. For seven days, they ate a huge feast and drank and partied until everyone was satisfied.

Elias was there to greet them as was Joshua. The disciples and the people treated Adam like a hero for saving them all. He was still having a hard time believing what had happened, though thankful God had used him.

Jesus made sure every person was healed of every sickness and disease. He used those seven days to teach his disciples many things about what to do after he was gone.

The disciples appointed 120 people to help baptize everyone. For six straight days, more than a million people were baptized in the sea. After they were finished with the feast and the baptisms, Jesus instructed everyone to meet him at the sea on the morning of the seventh day.

On the seventh day, Jesus stood up to speak. "I must leave you now."

The crowd groaned.

"I will not leave you alone. Receive the Holy Spirit."

Suddenly, a sound from heaven like a roaring windstorm filled the air. The Holy Spirit descended upon everyone. So much joy filled their hearts they seemed drunk. No one had been drinking; the sun had just come up, and it was only nine in the morning.[1]

Jesus turned to his disciples and spoke something to each one. No one else heard what was said to each one, but when Jesus finished, they all embraced and kissed. The disciples knew Jesus was leaving them again and they shed a myriad of tears as they said goodbye.

Jesus apparently saved his last goodbye for Adam. He turned to Adam and took him in his arms.

"I'm so proud of you. Look at how far you have come since your time on Earth."

"Lord," Adam said. "I'm going to miss you."

His stomach churned, his cheeks flushed, his heart literally hurt from the pain of losing his dearest friend he'd ever known for close to four hundred years.

"Don't be sad, Adam. Be of good cheer. You'll see me again."

"How can I be happy when you'll be gone? I went through so much to get here."

He looked out over the people. "I love the people, but I don't know what more I can do to help them. Will they ever really accept me as one of their own?"

"We will accept you," Lucas said. "We love you. Look at all the people. They adore you. You're our brother in Christ."

Jesus stepped away from Adam and said, "I have to go." He looked up to the sky.

A wave of panic rushed over Adam. Then he had an idea.

"Jesus!" Adam shouted. He wanted to go with him.

Jesus looked at Adam and nodded as if to reassure him it would be okay. Adam turned to Elias and hugged him. Elias raised his eyebrows. He had a surprised look on his face, unsure why Adam was saying goodbye, but he hugged him back.

Jesus reached out His hand toward Adam and motioned for him to come to him.

Adam excitedly ran over to Jesus. Jesus took his arm.

Suddenly, Jesus and Adam rose in the air. Jesus had one arm raised toward heaven and another arm securely holding Adam.

Adam looked down, and the people were becoming smaller and smaller as they rose faster and faster.

He'd experienced the same feeling during the liftoff of his spacecraft many years ago, but this was different. No words could describe what he felt as he was being swept into space without the benefit of a spacecraft surrounding him.

It all happened so fast, he wasn't able to take it all in. They were traveling even faster than any spacecraft Adam had ever been on.

All at once, the skies opened, and they ascended through the clouds. Adam could no longer see below. Jesus gently sat Adam down on a street made of gold. Adam knew from what he read in the Bible that he was in heaven.

The gate to heaven was made of diamonds and pearls. Beautiful stones glistened in the light. He'd heard of the pearly gates, but this gate was shinier and more luxurious than he'd imagined.

Jesus led Adam through the gate and immediately flew away.

Adam could see Jesus at a distance, sitting down on a throne at the right hand of God.

Heaven was more majestic than even the garden of Eden had been. Fragrant flowers and scents Adam had never experienced before. His senses were overwhelmed by the sights and sounds of something beyond even the possibility of human imagination.

The streets of gold were lined with mansions made of crystal and ivory. Those must be the mansions Jesus prepared for everyone.

The flowers, trees, and shrubs were alive, dancing and singing praises to God. Even the stones were crying out praises to God and were rejoicing. Laughter and singing permeated the air. Fountains of water cascaded through the city, shimmering from the light.

Everything was light. Bright, glorious light. Adam had never seen such bright lights.

Peace ... Calm ... Tranquility. Adam had never felt such peace.

Singing everywhere. Children and animals playing.

Adam looked at his hands. Glowing ...

The same crown of glory that was on Elias and the people in the garden was on Adam. His earthly body was gone, replaced by a spiritual body. No longer clothed, he was adorned with the glory of God radiating from every part of his body.

No pain. Neither physical, emotional, nor spiritual. On Earth, he felt constant physical aches and pain and continual uneasiness. He didn't even realize how horrible it had been until now, when it left him completely.

No sadness. No fear. Anger ... Resentment. Unforgiveness. Bitterness. Regret. All gone.

Total and complete release from his earthly body. Adam had become a spirit being and could see and feel the difference.

Overwhelming love filled every part of his being. He could tell something was different. He no longer had his sinful nature. He was no longer in the presence of constant evil. On Earth, he hadn't even realized how strong it was until now, when it was gone.

Adam could see the people in heaven from a distance. They had spiritual bodies like his. The same glow surrounded them that surrounded him. The glow of the people intensified the lights and created beams of light that bounced off of the mansions and radiated off what was the bluest sky he'd ever seen.

One big light shone off in the distance. Adam immediately fell to his knees. The glory of God illuminated everything in heaven. As glorious as the Garden of Eden had been, it didn't compare to heaven.

The beauty and perfection of heaven were beyond words, and Adam couldn't adequately describe it. He simply stood there taking it all in.

Someone called his name. He turned to look in the direction from which he heard the familiar voice.

Courtney and his daughter Jamie were walking toward him with huge smiles.

As they came closer, they began flying toward him.

He started to run toward them but was lifted into the air and instinctively flew in their direction, bridging the gap in almost no time.

He took them in his arms and held them tightly. The first time to meet Jamie face-to-face and touch her, feel her presence.

"I wasn't sure you were going to make it," Courtney said.

Adam laughed, "There were many times I didn't think I was going to make it either."

"We're so glad you're here. We have so many things to tell you," Jamie said enthusiastically.

Adam felt a touch on his shoulder. He turned.

Andrea . . . Of course, you would be here.

Andrea was his ex-wife. Jamie's mother. She kissed Adam and they embraced for several seconds. Adam didn't know how long. There was no time in heaven.

All four cried tears of joy. They took Adam by the arm and started walking.

"Where are we going?" Adam said.

"To show you your mansion. It's a big one," Courtney said.

"Then you're coming to our house," a voice behind them said loudly. "We're going to throw you a big party."

Adam turned to see who was speaking.

Adam and Eve were walking toward them with huge smiles on their faces.

SCRIPTURE REFERENCES

Chapter Five
1. John 2:4 2. Romans 3:23 3. John 10:18 4. John 8:10

Chapter Six
1. John 20:29

Chapter Seven
1. 1 Corinthians 1:27 2. Hebrews 9:22 3. Romans 3:10 4. John 15:13 5. Matthew 7:13-14 6. John 3:16 7. Romans 10:9 8. Romans 10:13-17

Chapter Eight
1. 2 Corinthians 5:7

Chapter Nine
1. Isaiah 1:18 2. Mark 9:35 3. John 15:13 4. Matthew 9:12

Chapter Ten
1. Matthew 26:53 2. John 4:49 3. Luke 8:45 4. Romans 8:1 5. 2 Corinthians 5:17 6. Romans 10:11

Chapter Eleven
1. Luke 17:22-24 2. Philippians 4:19 3. Matthew 14: 13-21 4. John 6:35 5. John 4:13-14 6. Luke 10 7. Matthew 10:15 8. John 14:12 9. Luke 6:27 10. Luke 6:29 11. 1 John 4

Chapter Twelve
1. Matthew 10:28 2. Acts 5:35-39

Chapter Thirteen
1. Acts 6:15 2. Revelation 2:21-22 3. Acts 7: 59-60 4. Matthew
27:3-5 5. John 1: 38-44

Chapter Fourteen
1. 2 Kings 9:10 2. Mark 10:17-31 3. Mark 9:29 4. John 3:16 5. John
3:1-21 6. Luke 5:20-26 7. John 14:6 8. Matthew 8:4 9. Romans 6:12
10. Hebrews 11:1 11 Matthew 22:37-39

Chapter Fifteen
1. Acts 9:1-19 2. James 5:14-16 3. Hebrews 12:2

Chapter Sixteen
1. Romans 3:23 2. Matthew 16:18 3. Matthew 14: 22-23 4. John
11:35 5. John 16:6 6. Luke 22:14-30 7. Ephesians 2:8-9

Chapter Seventeen
1. Luke 22:14-30 2. John 7:33 3. John 16:22 4. Matthew 26:38
5. Hebrews 13:8 6. Ecclesiastes 1:9 7. Romans 7:15 8. Luke 22: 1-4

Chapter Eighteen
1. Luke 29:34 2. John 19:30 3. John 20:29

Chapter Nineteen
1. Psalm 30:5 2. John 20:22 3. Romans 10:9 4. Exodus 14:11
5. Matthew 17:20 6. Exodus 14

Chapter Twenty
1. Acts 2

Thank you for purchasing this novel from best-selling author Terry Toler. As an additional thank you, Terry wants to give you a free gift.

Sign up for:

Updates
New Releases
Announcements

At terrytoler.com

We'll send you an eBook, *The Book Club*, a Cliff Hangers novella, free of charge. The one that started the Cliff Ford mysteries.

READ MORE BOOKS FROM TERRY TOLER

The Eden Stories

Read all the books in the series including The Longest Day which started the franchise. Click on the link below to see all the planet books.

The Eden Stories (8 book series) Kindle Edition (amazon.com)

Jamie Austen Thrillers

Read all the Jamie Austen Thrillers. They must be good. They've been number one on Amazon in ten different countries. Click on the link below.

THE JAMIE AUSTEN THRILLERS (12 book series) Kindle Edition (amazon.com) https://amzn.to/3vmPUy7

Cliff Hangers Mystery Series

Who wants to read a good mystery? We've got you covered! Read the Cliff Hangers where homicide detective, Cliff Ford, solves crimes in Chicago, with help from his wife Julia. These books have everything Terry Toler is known for. Page turning suspense, a hint of romance, and an ending you won't see coming.

The Cliff Hangers Mystery Series (4 book series)

Kindle Edition (amazon.com)
https://amzn.to/36WX3go

About Terry

Terry Toler is an Amazon international # 1 best-selling and award winning author. He writes clean fiction with a message and life changing nonfiction. He's a public speaker, entrepreneur, and has authored more than forty books.

Sign up for his newsletter where you'll get free stuff, exclusive content, and news of releases and promotions. He can be followed at terrytoler.com.

If you like his books, please take a few minutes to leave a review on Amazon. We really appreciate it. It helps draw more readers to his books. Thanks!

www.ingramcontent.com/pod-product-compliance
Lightning Source LLC
Chambersburg PA
CBHW022125170626
46808CB00002B/850